THE
YEAR
WE
FELL
FROM
SPACE

AMY SARIG KING

Published in the UK by Scholastic Children's Books, 2020
Euston House, 24 Eversholt Street, London, NW1 1DB, UK
A division of Scholastic Limited

London – New York – Toronto – Sydney – Auckland
Mexico City – New Delhi – Hong Kong

SCHOLASTIC and associated logos are trademarks and/or
registered trademarks of Scholastic Inc.

First published in the US by Scholastic Inc., 2019

Text © Amy Sarig King, 2019
Interior art © Nina Goffi, 2019

The right of Amy Sarig King and Nina Goffi to be identified as the author and
illustrator of this work has been asserted by them under the Copyright, Designs
and Patents Act 1988.

ISBN 978 0702 30193 3

A CIP catalogue record for this book is available from the British Library.

Printed by CPI Group (UK) Ltd, Croydon, CR0 4YY
Papers used by Scholastic Children's Books are made
from wood grown in sustainable forests.

1 3 5 7 9 10 8 6 4 2

www.scholastic.co.uk

THE YEAR WE FELL FROM SPACE

For Nick

I would rather be a superb meteor, every atom of me in magnificent glow, than a sleepy and permanent planet.

— JACK LONDON

It is not great telescopes that make great astronomers.

— MAX ERNST

Prologue — The Day We Fell

Mom and Dad sat Jilly and me down when we got home from school on a Friday. It was January cold outside — snow piled up on the edges of the quarter-mile-long lane to our house — and Dad made us hot chocolate when we got inside after our walk from the bus stop. Then, we sat on the red couch. They sat on the green one.

Mom said, "Dad and I are going to separate. He's going to move out this weekend. I'm sure you've noticed things aren't going well between us. We're sorry you've had to hear us fighting so much. But the main thing for you to know is that you'll still see both of us and that we both love you very much."

"You'll still see me all the time," Dad said. "I'm going to get some bunk beds so you can stay with me whenever you want." He didn't look us in the eyes. He was staring at the carpet, mostly.

"We want you to talk to us about anything that's on your mind and don't be afraid of the feelings you have about this because whatever you feel, it's totally normal," Mom said.

I wasn't afraid of the feelings I was having. In order, they were: relief, confusion, and fear. Probably some other ones, too, but those were the big ones. Jilly was pure sadness. Her body shook. I moved closer to her on the couch and put my arm around her.

Dad said, "Look, this is all my fault. I'm so sorry. We're going to do the best we can to make things right and try to be a family again."

And that changed everything. For example, my feelings rearranged themselves into: confusion, fear, and more confusion. Jilly shook less and her eyes widened as if she could somehow see our family not breaking apart. But she knew it was. I knew it was. Mom knew it was. Dad seemed to be the only one there who was unaware.

He was just saying stuff to make it seem better and to make Jilly not cry. Welcome to my life.

Example 1: Jilly and me in the back seat every summer while Dad drives us home from day camp. I ask if we can stop for ice cream. Dad says no. I go back to watching the trees pass by as we drive. Jilly starts to cry. She says something like "I really want ice cream!" and Dad stops for ice cream.

Example 2: It's summer vacation last year and Mom is hiking with her friend Patty. I ask Dad if Jilly and I can stay up late to watch an episode of *Star Trek*. He says no. I start heading up the stairs to brush my teeth and go to bed. Jilly cranks up the waterworks and says something like "But I really wanted to see it! And it's summer vacation!" and Dad turns on *Star Trek* and calls for me to come down.

It was always the same. I tried crying but he'd tell me that "this is just the way things are." For me. But not for Jilly. Jilly didn't have a *way things are*. She just got what she wanted as if her tears and my tears were two different elements.

He's not a bad dad. He's just mixed up, is all. When he's outside, he's usually fine. When he's inside, it's like he can't think right due to a lack of fresh air or something. It was winter. We were spending a lot of time inside.

Mom said, "Dad's going to get some help. You know he's been having some problems. He needs some time to figure things out."

I noted the *some*s in her sentences. Some help. Some problems. Some time.

Jilly said, "Figure out if he loves us."

Dad said, "Don't worry, baby. I'll be back."

Mom said, "Jack, don't say that. We talked about this already."

Dad said, "Sorry. But it's what I want." He turned to us and said, "Your mother is making me do this."

With that, Mom threw her hands into the air and plopped down on her favorite chair and crossed her arms.

....

This was the dance of my parents. Dad always led. Mom had to follow or else. It sounds bad and it was bad. I had just turned twelve the month before and I couldn't remember a time when they weren't fighting every other weekend. But it wasn't fighting, exactly. Dad would just start yelling and

Mom would try to keep it from us. Parents are weird to think they can hide yelling from people in their own house. Yelling is like a smoke alarm. And the point of a smoke alarm is to wake people up.

I knew this conversation was coming. Or I'd hoped. But I'd miss Dad, too. It was complicated.

Dad moved out that night. Mom's friend came to take me and Jilly out for dinner and ice cream. When we came home, Mom was there alone and Jilly cried for a while, but I didn't.

....

So now you know how it started, our fall from space. It's a long journey from up there to down here, and there are other things you need to know:

1. The stars aren't just stars, like you were taught. They tell me how I'm feeling when I look at them. No one can change my mind about this because no one knows anything about how big and powerful the universe is.

2. My dad is a good guy with a bad disease. He is not his disease. But sometimes he can seem it.

3. My dad was my guiding star for my whole life. It wasn't that I didn't like my mom. I love her. She's my mom. But Dad and I had something special. He and Mom always said we were cut from the same cloth.

4.   This is a problem.

5.   Picture this: I was nine years old and my dad and I were walking through the forest and we saw a doe and her two fawns only a few feet from us and then a buck walked up and that never happens. Dad was holding my hand and we froze and watched and it was the most beautiful thing I ever saw. A family of four. Just like the family pictures we had all over our house. The doe and her fawns moved away from the buck and Dad and the buck were staring at each other and Dad smiled and breathed deep, and the buck looked like he was going to walk over to us and then he bolted and ran deep into the woods.

Picture this: Dad had tears running down his cheeks and we just stood there holding hands and saying things like "Wow" and "Holy cow" and the tears kept coming from his eyes and after a minute, I didn't know if Dad was happy or sad but I knew he was my dad and I'd be there for him forever and he'd be there for me forever, too.

Picture this: Everything changed and I don't know why.

Part One:

THINGS FALL FROM SPACE

Chapter 1 – Pretend Pie

Mom's scribbling numbers again. The kitchen table is full of papers. Bills, booklets, yellow legal tablets. She's got the look of concentration, which can look like she's angry, but she's not.

Mom's always been a great communicator. She talks to the bill people on the phone as if she's known them for years—remembers their names, laughs, and cracks jokes. Jilly has picked up her signature closing—that part where the bill person asks if they can do anything else for you.

"Can you buy yourself a pie on the way home from work and pretend I made it for you?"

I've heard her say this a hundred times since I was little.

Jilly says it, too, but she doesn't have to pay bills or talk on the phone. She just says it to people working behind fast food counters and that guy at the car wash once. They always laugh because Jilly is funny.

Was. Jilly *was* funny.

....

I'm doing my usual thing for a Friday after school. No homework, I'm looking forward to a weekend of making new constellations. Since Mom's been taking up the kitchen table for two months with her divorce action station, I lay my newest star map out on the coffee table in the living room.

I have most of the stars drawn in, but no lines yet. I only connect the dots once the map is done. Making the new constellations is the most important part. The stars are always the same, but the lines and shapes change depending on how I'm feeling and what the sky is trying to tell me, which is why it's important for me to draw the maps. Sometimes I don't know how I'm feeling. The stars help me figure it out.

"I want to play a game or something," Jilly says. She's standing at the bottom of the stairs holding the stuffed tiger she hasn't let out of her sight for sixty-three days.

I look at my map and she stands there staring at me.

"What?" I ask.

"Are you going to play or what?"

I look at the clock on the wall. It's two hours until sundown. "Want to go outside?" I ask.

"No."

"Come on. It's finally spring. You can't stay cooped up in here forever," I say.

I look back at my map. Stars everywhere—big dots and little dots. I'm starting to see new shapes and I need time to figure out what they are.

Mom says, "Girls, I'm on the phone, okay?" Mom looks at me and crinkles her forehead. It's a signal. She moves her head toward the back door. Another signal.

As if it's my responsibility to get Jilly out of the house.

I roll up my map and put it on the top bookshelf.

"I'll race you to the stream," I whisper. "Put your shoes on."

"No," Jilly says. She's clutching her tiger so hard now, I'm afraid his stuffing will bust out.

I know not to fight her on this. I know what happens.

I grab a deck of cards from the shelf and take her up to my room.

I live in the attic now. Biggest room in the house. A little cold in the winter and a little hot in the summer, but who cares because it's the closest room to the stars.

Chapter 2 — Exciting Exceptions

Three hands of cards later, Jilly and I are at the kitchen table and Mom is dishing out Chinese food. Her paperwork is all stacked up on the windowsill where it will stay for the weekend.

The three of us share the lo mein and Mom and I share her spicy chicken because Jilly hates spicy things. She loves those thick noodles, though, and she slurps them up and makes us laugh. Or she used to. Now she just rolls them around her fork and eats them like this is some sort of business meeting.

Mom slurps her noodle and makes us laugh, but Jilly still won't slurp.

"How's your new map coming?" Mom asks.

"Good," I say.

"Connecting anything yet?"

"I see a few things. A rocking horse. A basketball court. A tiger." These aren't the things I see, but I say it anyway because weekends and take-out food are kinda sacred around here now.

"A tiger? Like mine?" Jilly points to her tiger, who is sitting on the windowsill guarding Mom's paperwork.

"Nah. I just said that so you'd look happy," I say.

Jilly stops looking happy.

Mom makes that face with her lips tight in a half smile, like she's saying *shucks* or a more grown-up version of it.

"Jilly and I are going to watch *The Wizard of Oz* tonight," Mom says.

"I'm going up to the hill," I say.

It's been cloudy or raining for three days. Atmospheric interference. It's when clouds get between me and the most important project of the twenty-first century.

I'm not bragging. And I'm not being dramatic. I'm serious.

I'm Liberty Johansen and I'm going to change the way people look at the night sky. I'm going to free them of old-constellation rules and teach them how to draw their own maps because the sky is trying to tell them something . . . only they don't know it yet because I'm a sixth grader and nobody ever listens to sixth graders who say they're going to do big things. But I'm an exception.

We're a family of exceptions.

I'm going to change the way the world looks at the stars even though I'm a girl and I live in a time where people laugh at science and girls and anything else that makes sense.

Jilly is a girl who has stopped going outside and who, at age nine, carries a stuffed tiger with her everywhere even though she's too old to do that.

And Mom is happier since Dad moved out even though everyone thinks she should be sad and lonely.

Exceptions are a lot more exciting than rules.

When I look up at the stars, I don't try to find constellations or boring old stuff like that. I see patterns. I see pictures. I see possibilities.

For example, if you take the dots on my map and compare them to a map of our town, we live on Polaris. We always point north and we help sailors and adventurers and lost hikers find their way. That's our job as Polaris. The North Star. Always right. Always consistent. Always asking you to buy a pie and pretend we made it for you.

Dad lives on Porter Drive now, which is about two miles from here. There isn't a star marking his new house. It's just all black sky. No pretend pie. No helping anyone find their way.

Chapter 3 — Postal Code Polaris

Polaris isn't hard to find if you know how to find it.

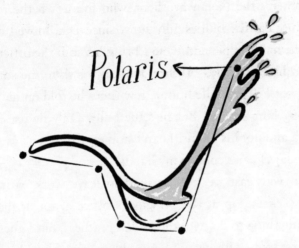

Polaris ←

Start with the Big Dipper, inside the old constellation Ursa Major. See a soup ladle, see the cup at the end of the handle. Follow that line up, out of the ladle, soup splashing twice its height, and you'll find us: bright, dependable Polaris. Guiding you to where you're going.

It's our job here on Polaris to nudge gently until you get there.

Unless you're Mom.

Mom is not a gentle nudge.

She has freak-outs sometimes but I can see why she has them. Jilly and I shouldn't really put tape on the walls. We shouldn't leave our paper scraps on the carpet she just vacuumed. And I probably shouldn't get in trouble so much in school.

....

Usually, it's the Nolan brothers, who live down the road from us. Patrick bullies Jilly now, since Dad moved out, and she never tells on him, so I bring her into the office to tell on him. Patrick's brother, Finn, is a jerk to me sometimes but I can handle him. A few times he told on me for pushing him around. But he's the bully. Only he uses his mouth and not his hands. I can't stop myself. I don't know. Some days I can't control my hands.

Anyway, last week Mom had to leave work early to come pick me up at the principal's office again. It didn't have anything to do with the Nolan brothers, but I guess it did have to do with me not being able to control my hands.

She's always calm in there. She says things that impress Ms. S., the principal.

"Lib, you can't keep blaming your behavior on other people," she said last week. "You have to own what you do. If you don't learn this soon you're going to have a heck of a time in middle school."

The principal nodded but I knew she'd given up on me in fourth grade when I kicked Ethan McGarret in the privates. It was self-defense, mind you, but I still probably shouldn't have done it.

Plus, last time I was in there was January, during the week we fell from space. Since then, even I've given up on me.

Mom kept talking. "Listen to me. It's no secret that this kind of family stuff causes some kids to act out. But seriously, what were you thinking?"

What was I thinking? I was thinking that the science wing hallway walls were too boring. I was thinking they needed a little panache. I only drew the best constellations. They were pretty.

Mom added, "I know you love the stars, kid, but save the drawings for your maps, okay?"

The drive home was quiet and I missed Dad. Dad would have understood why I drew stars on the science wing wall. He used to tell me things were going to be okay at times like that. He approved of what he called "sticking it to the man," which was what I was feeling when I drew the constellations on the science wing wall. Dad would have been proud of me. And he wouldn't have cared how good he sounded in front of Ms. S.

Now he's just living by himself and doesn't have to take care of anything. Not even mowing the lawn outside of his apartment. Not even us. It's been sixty-three days since we started our free fall from space and I haven't seen him once even though he said we'd see him all the time. Just dark sky, like he got sucked into a black hole.

So Mom freaks out sometimes. And Jilly can't go outside anymore. And I draw maps and more maps and more maps—even on the walls of the science wing.

Chapter 4 — Postal Code Polaris with a Faint Red Glow

Sundown is the best time of day.

Twilight.

Crepuscule. That's a real word. It means twilight.

Best time of day.

I get my newest map, a few pencils, and my blanket. "I won't be too long," I say as I head to the hill.

The hill is right behind our house. It's not really our house—we rent it from an old guy named Lou. It's a 1700s log cabin, now covered in ugly beige siding, built in the middle of fifty acres of woods. The hill is clear of trees, though, so the view of the night sky is big. It's not a steep hill, so it's easy to get to, and Lou keeps the trail cleared all year round.

At the top, there's a small, flat clearing. When it's warmer, Mom and Dad let me sleep out here. Some people think it's weird for me to sleep outside but Mom and Dad used to be hike guides and survival skills teachers. They lived along the Appalachian Trail for years. It's how they met. They don't agree on much anymore, but they will always agree that sleeping outside is good for you.

I lay my blanket out and get ready to see each star pop out from its hiding place and wish on the first one.

For the first forty days after Dad moved out I sat bundled in my snow clothes and wished Mom and Dad would get back together, but I don't think that's going to happen. For the last twenty-three days I didn't know what to wish for. Tonight is different. I know what to wish for.

....

There's a screech owl out here somewhere. She screeches me to sleep every night, even in winter. Twilight is when she's just waking up. I whisper, "Good morning, owl."

Mars is already visible in the western sky. Can't miss her. She glows a faint red and in my mind she misses Venus. Even though the two planets don't always travel together, I have this memory of when Dad first pointed them out to Jilly and me. Three years ago, we took a walk every night to see them — Venus brighter than anything in the night sky and Mars to her right, glowing red. Like Jilly and me, we said that night. Jilly is Venus. I'm Mars. I'm glowing faint red.

I don't know what I'm so angry about. Mom is a good mom. Jilly is annoying now that she doesn't go outside anymore, but I can handle her. School is weird but I'm dealing with it okay. I wish they hadn't asked me to wash my constellations off the science wing wall. I wish they would have asked me to draw more of them. Maybe that's what I'm angry about.

Sirius is the first star, right above me in the south sky.

I say the poem about first-star-I-see-tonight and then I think hard about my wish.

If I told you the wish, it wouldn't come true, so you'll just have to wait to find out.

Rigel is the next star to show itself. Then Capella, then Betelgeuse. Slowly they all show themselves and Orion's belt pops up between Rigel and Betelgeuse. I start to name the old constellations I know. Taurus, right where Mars is, Orion, of course, Cancer and Gemini right next to each other, and Leo to the left of them. And the Big Dipper, the soup ladle that helps you find Polaris the North Star, is right above my head.

I pull out my map and face the opposite direction of Polaris because it's the southern sky that's been confusing me on this map. South—direction of Porter Drive where Dad now lives. Without us. Nothing confusing about that.

I have a headlamp—the kind cave hikers wear—and I slip it on my head and stare at the map. I've left a big space where Leo should be. I look back at the sky to find the dots I need, but the sky is lit up in an odd way, as if someone has turned the sun back on. I turn off my headlamp and there's a shooting star. Right then.

People say shooting stars are rare, but they're not. I see one every week.

This one moves all the way through the sky, from east to west—it's slower than most shooting stars I've seen and doesn't seem to be burning out. And then it makes a turn. It looks like it's coming right at me.

I glance at my map again and make a pencil mark for Regulus, which is the brightest star of Leo. When I look back up, the shooting star is still there. But brighter. Closer. Slower. Aiming straight for me. I shake my head because I know that can't be true. Things don't just fall from space.

But sometimes they do.

But they don't here.

Or maybe they do. I don't know.

Because this one is coming right for me, on top of this hill, and I start to wonder if I'm going irrational like Dad did.

Chapter 5 — Liberty Johansen Is Not Going Irrational

It's brighter than the sun. That's all I know. It's blinding and I can't move. I sit on my blanket and stare at it through my fingers. The sound is there—like a jet and a storm rolled into one. I swear the ground is shaking.

Liberty Johansen, you are not going irrational.

The light comes closer and I don't know what to think. I don't know what to do. I try to remember everything Dad ever taught me about meteors and meteorites, but I don't remember anything. Or, what I do remember is too scary to think about . . . so I run through vocabulary words.

An asteroid is a small rock orbiting the sun. A meteoroid is a small part of a comet or asteroid. A meteor is the light show a meteoroid makes when it passes through Earth's atmosphere—a shooting star. A meteorite is a meteoroid that makes it through the atmosphere and lands on Earth.

This is a meteor. A light show. A trick. That's all it is. But the ground is still shaking and I know it's not in my imagination because the screech owl has stopped screeching and the trees are making a sound like wind and there's no wind and the light is so bright. So bright. And there's a trail of smoke behind the light.

An airplane has gone on fire and is about to crash. A

satellite component is falling to Earth. Liberty Johansen, this is not a spaceship.

BOOM!

The air is knocked out of my lungs. I can't breathe right. I think I hear glass breaking, but I'm not sure where and I could be imagining it. Before I can figure out what to do, there's a bright flash.

The flash lasts longer than the boom. When I look back up, everything is dark again. I can breathe, but I'm so scared, I'm barely breathing at all.

I think I just went irrational.

But then something small, like a pebble, falls from the sky and hits me on my head and lands in my lap.

I cover my head with my arms and only then can I hear Mom yelling for me. I try to yell back but between the lack of air in my lungs and the fact that I'm temporarily frozen, I can't say anything at all.

"Lib! Liberty!" Mom calls.

I hear her at the base of the path to the hill. "Liberty! Answer me! Come home!"

I hear her run back, sneakers crossing the deck, and the sliding door open and then close again. Then I hear something above me in the tree limbs—like something is falling fast—the same way it sounds when deer run through the woods. Branches crack and twigs fall.

There's a thud. It's loud. It's to my right, down the hill a bit. It sounds like the time I fell off the monkey bars at recess. Thud. Something heavy.

I don't want to move.

I don't want to move until I know what just happened.

I don't want to move until I know for sure an alien isn't waiting for me, ready to take me back to its spaceship and dissect me. I still can't see right. I blink a few times. I stare up and try to find Mars to get my bearings. It's there, glowing a faint red.

I stand up and try to figure out what just happened.

This isn't what I wished for.

I shine my headlamp toward where the thud noise came from. Something new is in the woods. I think it's a meteorite. A lot bigger than the one that hit me on the head. I picture it glowing red, like Mars and me. I can't tell how big it is, but I know it can't be too big because if it was even the size of a small car when it was in space, and it fell, there's a good chance I'd be dead. And Mom and Jilly. And Lou and his wife, Veronica, who live up the lane. We'd all be dead. I know that.

I know it was probably moving hundreds of thousands of miles per hour when it hit the ground. I know it's not really glowing red, but my eyes are making it seem that way in the lamplight. I stay rational. That's the pie I bought when Dad left. I've been pretending Mom made it for me all this time, but really I made it myself. Rational pie.

Chapter 6 – Aliens

"What the heck was that?" Jilly says when I walk in the door.

"No idea," I say.

"You didn't see it?" she asks.

Mom is busy looking at the two kitchen windows that are missing chunks of glass and sweeping the floor with a broom to catch the pieces. "Jilly, go sit down. You don't have any shoes on."

"Was it a spaceship?" Jilly asks.

I shake my head.

"Did something crash?"

"I don't know," I say.

"You look weird."

"I feel weird."

"Maybe you got adducked by aliens."

"Abducted," Mom corrects from the kitchen.

I say, "It was probably a meteorite. Sometimes bigger ones break through Earth's atmosphere."

"How do we know you're telling the truth? Maybe they brainwashed you." Jilly smiles.

"I like when you're funny," I say.

She frowns.

I feel the small meteorite in my pocket. I roll it between my fingers and my thumb. Something about it makes me feel okay.

....

Lou, our landlord, comes driving down the lane in his truck. He parks and then he's suddenly in our house. When Dad lived here, Lou would knock first and wait.

"Well, I'll be," he says, looking at the pile of glass on the kitchen floor. "I've seen a lot of things. Never saw a storm that fast."

"Liberty thinks it was a meteorite," Mom says. Jilly is jumping up and down to get Lou's attention, but he's in the kitchen and she's stuck barefoot in the living room until Mom is sure all the glass is cleaned up.

"Would have had to be a big meteor!" he laughs.

"I was out there," I say. "I watched it."

He turns to me and makes that face like he's impressed.

I say, "It's not like it's snowing."

He nods. Lou's a hunter. I think he likes that I hang out on his hill and that I like nature. I don't like that he kills animals and mounts their heads on his wall, but I guess people have to do whatever makes them happy.

"I think it was aliens," Jilly says. "Coming down to see if humans are worth talking to."

Lou says, "If you were an alien, would you think we were worth talking to?"

"Some of us, maybe," Jilly says.

"Sweetheart, if the aliens met you first, I bet they'd think we were worth it," Lou says. Then he turns to Mom and says, "I'll go get the cardboard."

Jilly takes her place on the couch and we listen to Mom telling Lou she can tape the windows up herself. She has to insist. Lou doesn't say anything dumb this time about Dad not being here to help. He just leaves the cardboard in the kitchen and drives away in his truck.

Chapter 7 — We Need to Talk about Dad

It's not like I'm trying to keep it a secret. People don't like to talk about this kind of stuff. Especially not to kids because they think we'll get big ideas in our heads or that we'll worry. Of course, we worry anyway, so it's better that we know.

I don't know much.

I know Dad has depression. That he gets angry a lot. That he yells a lot. And then, after a day or two or four, he turns into an apology machine and acts like everything is fine.

You never know how long it will last.

You never know why it's happening.

Mom finally took him to a doctor two years ago — when I was Jilly's age — and they don't really talk to us about it.

So now you know what I know.

Which isn't much, like I said.

But I should tell you that on our night walks when I was little Dad and I used to make up songs about the stars so I could remember them better. By the time I was eight, I knew most of the old constellations. By the time I was nine, I was making my own. The stars were our thing. They were outside where Dad felt best, and they were bright, and dependable. Just like Dad on camping trips and in emergencies like when the power went out or a tree fell and blocked the driveway. He was great with all that. He wasn't very good with humans.

I don't know what aliens would think about humans if they came here. Humans are weird. We have some problems, I guess. I care more about stars than I care about humans anyway. Humans have been nothing but a pain in my butt so far. Which makes me more like Dad. And I'd be lying if I said that didn't worry me.

Chapter 8 — Things Change

Once Lou leaves, I want more than anything to go back out and see the meteorite, but when I pick up my unfinished star map and move toward the door, Mom says, "Can you skip it for tonight, Lib? Not sure what happened out there but I'm nervous."

I nod and put my map on the table.

Jilly says, "I'm tired," and flops into Mom's arms.

So Mom sends her to bed and reads her a story about dragons and when Mom comes back down, I help her tape up the second broken window.

....

In bed, I look at my star map. The dots connect and look like a broken window and one of Jilly's imaginary aliens.

The shapes change depending on what the stars want me to think about.

Before I went to the hill tonight, this map had the letter *R*, a book, and something round, like a ring.

Taped up on my ceiling, which is slanted because the attic is right under the roof, there are still three maps I never finished from winter. The dots are there but I could never see anything in them. Usually the shapes just pop out at me and I can see things clearly. But winter was hard. I think that's why I can't connect the dots.

I pick up the map from tonight and I connect dots for a spaceship, an alien, and a broken window. It takes me a few minutes, tops. No problem. I date and sign the map at the bottom. *March 22, 2019, Liberty Johansen.*

I get back into bed and stare up at the old maps from winter. I stand up a few times and make certain stars bigger dots. I tilt my head to either side and squint. Still no pictures or shapes or ideas pop out. Maybe that's the thing about bad winters. There are no connections. There's nothing you can do with the dots.

Chapter 9 – The Magic Box

SATURDAY, MARCH 23, 2019

Saturdays used to be fun.

We would clean our rooms early and then go places together and do things. Like the farmer's market or hiking at Hawk Mountain or maybe a trip to the lake to watch birds. Sometimes Dad would take us fishing. Sometimes Mom would take us out on the trails to test a new kind of boots they sent her from work. Mom tests boots. And backpacks. And camping stoves and tents and hatchets and just about anything they sell in the Outdoor World catalog, where she works. Sometimes Jilly and I would play all day outside on the swing set or in the woods or in the stream behind our house. Sometimes we'd climb into Lou's tree stands in the forest and pretend we were birds, high above everything else.

Now Jilly takes forever to clean her room on Saturday mornings and whines the whole time. Today Mom is using the magic box trick. The magic box trick is simple: *Put one hundred things in this box that do not give you joy.* That's how Mom says it. What she really means is: Put one hundred things in the box that you don't play with anymore, don't need, or don't want. Jilly wants and needs everything these days so today's magic box will take a while.

Now Mom has a second job writing about trails, national parks, and survival stuff for some hippy hiker website and she doesn't have as much time as she used to on weekends, so Jilly taking forever to fill the magic box is probably fine.

....

I go outside and to the hill and I wonder if I imagined everything from last night. *Sure, Liberty. A meteorite just fell from the sky into your yard, of all places.*

At the top of the hill I look down to see if it's still there. It's still there.

Sure, Liberty, there's a big meteorite in the woods. Okay.

But it happened. Just because some people won't believe me doesn't mean it didn't happen. I was there.

Most people have a hard time believing stuff.

That's the whole point of my star maps.

The Mayans saw different pictures in the sky. The Chinese have their own old star maps. Everyone does. Different shapes. Different names for each constellation. Why are we stuck with gods and bears and queens and warriors? I see toasters. I see hats and unicorns and ice skates. I see anything I want to see because all the sky gives us is dots. It's our job to connect them. Why would I connect them the same way some guy thousands of years ago did? They didn't even have electricity back then. They were still dying from diseases we don't even get anymore.

So maybe the science teacher doesn't like that I make up my own constellations. Who cares? Just because he doesn't like it doesn't mean I won't keep doing it.

And just because no one will believe a meteorite the size of a football landed in my woods doesn't mean it didn't happen.

I sit next to it and touch it. It's cold, same as any other rock. It's not the same color as other rocks around here, though. Mostly we have red rocks. Sometimes a bit of blue limestone. This thing is light brown like sand, and it has spots. It's smooth—almost as smooth as if it had been in a river for a hundred years or more. I don't know what to do with it. I can't leave it here. I can't hide it out here. I can't bury it.

It's the answer to the wish I made on the star even though I didn't ask specifically for any of this. Wishing on stars isn't like making a birthday list. Even if you're specific, the sky can send whatever it wants to help you because the sky is kinda mystical and old. It has different ideas about what we need.

Chapter 10 — The Crabby Professor

After lunch Mom says she's going to the grocery store and she asks Jilly to come with her but Jilly won't budge from the couch where she's reading a book and hugging the tiger. This means I have to stay here and babysit.

"Can I use the computer? I have to look some stuff up," I say.

"No computer while I'm out," Mom says.

"It's just star stuff," I say. "Research."

"No games, okay?" she says, then walks out the door.

I type *I think I found a meteorite* into the search engine and click the magnifying glass icon. There are 8,919,000 results.

The first thing I find is a list of meteorite facts. Meteorites attract magnets and are: very heavy, not radioactive, and sometimes have metallic flakes on their surface. The pictures make me think that wow — I had no idea meteorites could be so different from each other. There are ones that look like blobs of metal and ones that look like weird rocks. They're all different colors, not like rainbow colors or anything, but rock colors. Red, black, brown, gray — and some are shiny and some are dull.

I go back and click on the next page result and find a

page filled with capital letters. It starts with: YOU HAVE PROBABLY NOT FOUND A METEORITE.

I stare at that sentence and I'm scared to read more. But I stay on the page because this guy — a professor — seems to know what he's talking about.

NOT EVERY ROCK THAT FALLS TO EARTH IS A METEORITE.

JUST BECAUSE A ROCK WASN'T THERE YESTERDAY DOESN'T MEAN IT'S A METEORITE.

PLEASE DON'T CONTACT ME ABOUT YOUR SO-CALLED METEORITE.

Crabby guy, this professor. He has a list that's eighty-four sections long about "WHY YOUR DUMB ROCK ISN'T A METEORITE." The more I read, the more my rock fits the description of a meteorite.

I go back to my search results. I find a place that sells meteorites. I click on that. Who knew that there were meteorite necklaces for sale? And who knew that people sell meteorites for $20,000 or more?

I think about how I could buy a telescope with that money. A really good telescope, too — maybe one that can see Saturn's rings and the Orion Nebula. I think about how I could help Mom out with the bills or something more responsible. Like saving for college.

I think about writing Dad an email to tell him about it. He'd be so excited. But I don't.

"Wanna play a game?" Jilly asks.

"I'm researching."

"You're staring into space."

"That's part of research," I say. "I'm thinking."

"After you research, then?"

"Maybe. It's nice out today. Want to go swing?"

"No."

"Think about it. I have to go do something."

I grab a magnet off the fridge before I head out the door to the rock.

....

The magnet sticks. There's rust-colored metallic markings all over the surface. And when I try to pick it up, I can't. It's that heavy. Heavy as two Jillys. Heavier than me, and it's only the size of my head.

I'm no professor, but this is a meteorite.

I don't know why I doubted myself because I saw it fall from the sky. But I'm twelve. I'm an amateur creative astronomer. And I doubt myself all the time. If I didn't doubt myself, then I'd end up cocky like the Nolan brothers. Anything I could do to not be like them, I'd do it.

I walk back to the house and put the magnet in my pocket and it sticks to the tiny rock that hit me last night. Another meteorite.

I close my eyes and see my imaginary response to the crabby professor.

THE THING THAT FELL IN MY WOODS IS TOTALLY A METEORITE.

....

Once Mom comes home from the grocery store, our week-end is a blur of games and a movie and charades. Charades aren't as fun indoors as they are around a campfire, but it's cold out there. After Jilly goes to bed on Sunday, Mom helps me study for a math test. Fractions. Again. As if I can't remember what a common denominator is from the last three years of learning fractions. I get a few problems wrong because I'm distracted by the meteorite.

It's outside. I'm inside. But I can hear it calling to me.

Don't worry.

I'm fine.

I just like science, is all.

Part Two:

OTHER

PHENOMENA

IN

MY

GALAXY

Chapter 11 — The Nolan Brothers

On Monday morning, Patrick Nolan is whispering at the bus stop. He's saying things about lightning hitting our house on Friday night because we deserved it. Jilly grips her tiger more tightly and I give Patrick a look like he should shut up or else I'll rearrange his freckles.

This happens every other day when Patrick's mother can't drive him to school. But only since Dad moved out. Before then, Patrick was asking Jilly to marry him, or playing fun games with her in the woods, or sitting in our kitchen drinking hot chocolate after we all went sledding. Dad moving out changed everything with the Nolans.

Finally after another minute of Patrick whispering, Jilly starts to cry. Her eyes just leak water. And Patrick can see it so he starts whispering louder. He hisses, "Everyone knows a family needs a man."

I wish I hadn't heard that.

If I hadn't heard that, I wouldn't have to grab Patrick by the shoulders and say, "Shut up, you little jerk!"

And if I hadn't said that, Finn wouldn't have to pull me

off him and say, "Keep your hands off my brother, you feminist."

I'm not even in school yet and I already hate today.

....

We've been stuck with the Nolan brothers for as long as I can remember because we're the only kids who live this far out in the woods. Finn and I used to be friends, I guess, but the older he got, the more weird he got. It was normal boys-and-girls stuff starting around fifth grade. He didn't talk to me much anymore, and if he did, he kept things short and pretended like I didn't much matter to him anymore. And then since Dad moved out, he got kinda mean. Cold, really. I don't know. Finn's whole family was different. I never liked sitting in their kitchen when it was their turn to make post-sledding hot chocolate, never liked playing in their pool, and never liked being around when Mr. and Mrs. Nolan were there because it was too stressful. We had enough stress of our own at home.

I used to worry about Finn. He had bad days when we were younger, and he got in trouble a lot in school. I used to sit with him on the bus those days and he'd be so scared to go home. One time I made him come home with me because he couldn't stop shaking. That was third grade. Dad drove him home before dinner and when Dad came back, he looked so sad, it made me cry.

It's no secret that Mr. Nolan is not a nice man. I figure Patrick is only saying this stuff to Jilly because he heard it from his dad first. Patrick is worse even though he's the little brother. But now it's rubbing off on Finn. A few weeks ago, Finn told me that Mom should have let Dad do whatever he wanted because men are in charge and that's the way things are supposed to be.

At least Mom was dealing with it. She wasn't getting yelled at all the time and then curling her brain into a hedgehog ball like Mrs. Nolan would when Mr. Nolan was a jerk to her. I never felt safe in that house and Patrick and Finn are turning out just like their father. I already pity whoever they take to the prom.

As for Finn calling me a feminist, I don't think he knows what that word means. How could he know what it means growing up in a house like that?

Chapter 12 — Jilly and the Wet Tiger

By the time the bus drops us off at home, I didn't draw anything on the walls, didn't get called to the principal's office, didn't talk to anyone in my class, and I didn't have to see Finn Nolan on the bus because their mom always picks them up from school. Probably with warm homemade cookies and individual cartons of milk because Mr. Nolan says so.

It's drizzling and Jilly and I share her umbrella because I always forget mine at school. Jilly keeps talking about Patrick Nolan and how mean he is. I nod and listen, but really I'm thinking about the meteorite and how I have to get it out of the woods and into my room.

Mom's on the phone again when Jilly and I walk in. She holds up her finger to her lips for us to be quiet and she smiles and waves.

I put on my raincoat and go out to the woods. Jilly tries to chase after me, but she stops on the deck. Can't go any farther. She calls my name over and over again and I pretend not to hear her.

I start up the hill and I worry about Jilly because she's standing in the pouring rain but I don't ask her to come with me because I know it would be an hour-long conversation about how she can't go outside. I just want to see the meteorite. I'm allowed to have a life.

The rock is still here. It's still heavy. I try to pick it up but it's slippery in the rain and it thumps down into the mud again. I think. I think. I think.

I walk back down the hill and find Jilly three steps into the lawn, still holding her now-very-wet tiger and making a low sound in her throat. Like she's growling and crying at the same time.

Because Mom has asked us not to use the word *crazy* I can't tell her she looks crazy, but she does. "You're acting irrational," I say. But she can't hear me because she's babbling and crying. There's snot coming out of her nose and it forms a bubble and I feel bad.

"What are you two doing?" Mom says. She's in the doorway and looks a mix of confused and concerned.

"Just checking out something in the woods," I say.

"It's raining," Mom says.

Jilly answers, still growling, "YES, WE *KNOW* IT'S RAINING."

Silence.

This is when Mom and I both realize that this is the first time Jilly has been outside willingly in sixty-six days.

Mom says, "I'll make hot chocolate," and goes back inside.

Jilly says, "Why won't you play with me?"

"It's raining."

"What are you doing up there in the rain?"

"It's a long story. It's stupid," I say. "Come on. Let's go drink hot chocolate."

"I'm staying here."

"It's raining and cold! Come on. Hot chocolate."

"I'M STAYING HERE!" she yells. She throws her tiger in the mud and crosses her arms.

I try not to judge Jilly. She's going through something the way we're all going through something. And now the tiger is on the ground, Jilly is out of the house, and even though she's crying and acting irrational, this is progress.

"Do you want me to take tiger inside to dry off?"

She nods.

I have no idea how to explain this to Mom.

....

"What were you two doing out there?" she asks.

"I was checking on—um—the hill. I left my favorite pencil up there on Friday night."

"What's your sister doing?" she asks.

I look out the window. Jilly is on the swing set, swinging. In the rain. I point.

"Did you find it?" she asks.

I look confused because A. I forgot that I just lied about my pencil and B. Why isn't Mom worried about Jilly swinging in the rain? "Nah. I think it's probably with my star map," I say.

She looks at me and smiles.

I show her the soaking-wet tiger. "Can I put this in the dryer?"

"That thing needs to get washed. She hasn't let go of it since . . . in a long time."

"Since Dad moved out," I say. "You can say that."

She looks at the tiger, and then the floor. "Since Dad moved out."

....

I don't think there's anything wrong with Dad moving out. Today, I mean. He doesn't call us, he hasn't had us to his house yet, and he seems to have zero interest in coming back or being part of the family. Or part of anything. But I'd be lying if I said I wasn't worried.

He's arranged three weekend visits so far and canceled every one of them at the last minute. Mom has to deal with him on the phone. She tries her best to stay friendly because it's what she reads about couples with kids going through divorce. *Keep things civil. Stay as friendly as you can. Don't talk badly about each other in front of the children.*

Dad doesn't make it easy. When she talks about it, she says it's not entirely his fault. He's not well, she says. *He's not well.* By which she means Dad has to go to talk to psychiatrists and stuff.

I used to think people who saw psychiatrists were irrational, like in the old cartoons we have on DVD. But it turns out that a lot of people have to see psychiatrists. It's just because they need help with things.

Mom talks to a therapist named Rosemary every week on Wednesdays so she can get help with her new life without Dad. Jilly needs help with Dad leaving, so she talks to a child psychologist named Jan every week since he left. Mom's asked if I want to see Jan too and I've told her no. I'm fine.

When she gets back upstairs from putting the tiger in the wash, Mom asks me to sit and hands me a mug of hot chocolate.

"How was today?" Mom asks.

"It was all right."

"How are you feeling about Dad?" she asks. "Us, his depression, anything?"

This is complicated. Because it's not like they ever talked to us about what was really going on. It's always in some sort of code. *He's not well. He's having a bad day.*

Thing is, I still can't figure out why it was a good idea for Dad to move out. Like, when he got sick in the brain, he moved away from the only people who really cared for him. Sure, maybe there was something more that I was too young to understand, but the whole thing didn't make Mom look very nice.

"I do have a question," I say.

She sits.

"So Dad's family has it too, right?"

She nods. "It can run in families sometimes."

She tells me some vague stories about Dad's family. Nothing remarkable. I already knew all those stories already. While she talks, I wonder if maybe we should have gone with Dad and not stayed with Mom. Because if something happens to my brain, I don't want her to kick me out too.

Chapter 13 — Space in My Bedroom

When Jilly comes inside, it's as if she was never the other Jilly. Not the Jilly who yelled at Mom and me, and not the Jilly who was standing in the pouring rain by herself, with snot running down her chin. She looks like she'd meant to go swinging in the rain.

She's also freezing and Mom insists that she take a hot shower before dinner and follows her to her room to collect her wet clothes. I grab my toughest backpack — an Outdoor World Day Pack — and go to the hill.

For some weird reason when I get to the rock, I say, "Hello, rock."

I probably need more friends.

I move it from where it's stuck into the mud — about three inches deep — and open the backpack and roll it in. Once I zip the backpack, I squat and put the straps on my shoulders and then stand slowly. It's not as heavy on my back as it was in my arms, but I have to bend over to stay balanced.

Mom and Jilly are in the kitchen by the time I come in and even though Jilly is the nosiest sister ever, she's too pre-occupied by helping Mom make her magic meatloaf to notice that I have mud on my clothes and that I need the railing to pull myself and the rock up the stairs.

By the time I get up two flights to my bed in the attic room, my back hurts.

I sit for a minute and look around. I can't figure out where to put it.

"On the floor."

I don't know who said that, but I think I'm talking out loud to myself. Of course it should go on the floor. It weighs more than I do.

Next to my bed I have a bunch of old stuffed animals. I move them out of the way so they don't get any mud on them and I squat down so the backpack eases itself onto the floor. I unzip it and roll the rock out.

"Thanks."

"You're welcome."

I stand it up the way it landed and I wipe off the mud with a wad of tissues.

I arrange the animals around it so it has friends.

I change my clothes so I'm not covered in mud.

I hide the Outdoor World Day Pack under my bed until laundry day.

"Nice room," the rock says.

"Thanks," I answer.

....

At dinner, Mom asks us about school. Jilly has stories about the kids in her class and a game they played in gym. I don't really remember what we did in school. In school

I'm either thinking about the stars or divorce or the meteorite. Even before the meteorite or the divorce, my brain was always in space.

Dad always told me school isn't for everyone and that I have bigger things to think about. And it's not like I have close friends or any social life or anything. Some kids join band or play sports.

I just think about stars. Usually by myself.

I'm probably from another planet.

Chapter 14 — We Need to Talk about School, I Guess

The school year had already been weird before Mom and Dad sat us down that day in January.

Everyone in sixth grade was trying to be boyfriends and girlfriends. It seemed so silly. It made school harder — all the breakups and people taking sides and passing notes. Leah Jones told me when we got back from winter break that I had to stop talking to John, a kid I've known since second grade, because he broke some girl's heart. "If you talk to him, you're a traitor to womankind," she'd said. Leah Jones used to be my friend. I went to her birthday sleepovers every year for four years and we had a recess rock band in third grade. Sixth grade changed her and I still don't know why.

Anyway, I knew the breakup wasn't John's fault. His ex-girlfriend had dumped him for a kid from band who she liked more. I couldn't see how talking to John now made me a traitor to womankind, so I kept talking to him.

The womankind of sixth grade recess shunned me once they found out. And then they sent David. David kept asking me to be his girlfriend all through January until finally, on the Tuesday of the week we fell from space, I'd had enough.

"Look—you're a nice kid and everything—but I'm too young to have a boyfriend and I don't want a boyfriend. I don't even want you to want me to be your girlfriend. It makes me feel weird."

"So you don't like boys?" David said.

"I just don't like boyfriends and girlfriends."

"So you don't like anybody?" he asked.

"I just don't want to be your girlfriend, okay? You seem nice. Nothing wrong with you. But I don't want to do this dumb stuff like girlfriends and boyfriends. It's stupid."

"Are you going to Leah and Mike's wedding at recess tomorrow?"

I shook my head. "That's what I mean. We're in sixth grade. Having weddings is stupid."

"So you think weddings are stupid?"

It was the Tuesday after my dad moved out. Of course I thought weddings were stupid.

I didn't answer him because the recess teachers blew their whistles and we all went inside.

Later that day, a note appeared on my desk.

David told me that you think my marriage to Mike is stupid and that you think I'm stupid and that Mike is stupid. If you're so smart then why aren't you married yet? I can tell you why. Nobody likes you. No one will sit with you at lunch anymore and no one will talk to you. You're excommunicated from the sixth grade class. You can sit with Malik now and let him spit milk at you.

Leah—class president

We didn't have a class president yet—we were in sixth grade.

I didn't know what to think about the note. It didn't change my mind. If anything, it made the whole marriage-at-recess/boyfriends-and-girlfriends thing seem stupider. I worried about Leah, just like I worried about Finn Nolan. But it was as if they were traveling in two different directions. Finn got quieter and meaner and Leah got louder and meaner.

As for sitting with Malik for lunch, that was fine with me. I've always liked him—maybe more so because he has a life-threatening nut allergy and has to sit at a lunch table by himself. His mom and dad are from Iran, so Malik not only looks different from most of the kids at West El, but people treat him different, too. Not always mean, either. (Though—sometimes mean.) The music teacher loves the kid. Malik plays piano and one time during the talent show, the whole school thought he might be famous one day. That was before the milk incident, last year. Now people don't really talk to him. Their loss. Malik is hilarious.

Chapter 15 — Conversations with a Rock

Jilly goes outside now. She doesn't bring the tiger to school anymore. She still whines and cries to get her way sometimes, but I think that's just Jilly. Something is different, though, since last week when she went out in the rain. Something big.

"I want to call Dad," she says. Neither of us has called Dad since he left and he hasn't called us, either. She seems angry about this. I'm probably angry about it, too, but I also used to take silent walks with Dad in the forest. I like to imagine Dad's silence for the last two and a half months as a long walk in the woods, I guess.

Mom is out testing two new pairs of all-weather boots, a fleece vest, and a fitness tracker. I'm looking at the star map I drew this week and the shapes are forming.

Jilly repeats herself. "I want to call Dad."

"Go ahead," I say.

"Do you want to talk to him, too?" Jilly asks.

"Nah. I'm good."

She picks up the phone and I go to my room in the attic and I polish the meteorite.

That probably sounds all wrong and makes you worry about me. But I'm fine. The meteorite is just — I don't know. It's part of me or something. It's a sign that things are going to be okay one day.

I'd like to know what day, but it can't tell me.

All it can tell me is that everything is going the way it's supposed to.

Even when I hear Jilly raising her voice to Dad on the phone, I know that everything is going the way it's supposed to.

"You said we'd see you!"

"You didn't have to lie!"

"I don't care how it makes you feel!"

I'm glad Jilly can talk like that. I don't know what I'd say to Dad today if I talked to him.

"It doesn't make any sense that you tell us we're going to come over and then say we can't," she said. "And it's mean. We need you!"

The meteorite says, "I don't need him."

"Me neither," I say. "I don't need anybody."

The rock says, "Friends are nice, though."

"Friends? No."

"I'm your friend," the meteorite says.

"You can't turn on me," I say. "All my other friends turned on me."

The rock says, "Just Finn and Leah."

"Exactly."

"Leah's different, though," the rock says.

I don't say anything.

There's the sound of stomping. "You can't keep doing

this!" Jilly says to Dad on the phone. She's not crying or anything. She's just mad. I kind of envy her.

I can see Mom walking down one of Lou's trails. That gives Jilly a minute and thirty seconds to get off the phone. Unless she doesn't care if Mom hears her. I don't know what goes through her mind anymore. Since last week she's older than me in the way she acts. I mean, look at her. She's on the phone yelling at Dad and I'm in my room talking to a rock.

One of us is dealing with this the right way.

I don't think it's me.

I go downstairs and point toward where Mom is and mouth the word "Mom" to Jilly, who says, "We miss you and this isn't fair," and hangs up the phone. I go back to my star map. It looks like a man walking alone in the woods. While Mom takes off her boots on the bench outside, Jilly face-plants on the red couch and I draw the shapes of my week into the map. The trees are enormous above the man. There are so many of them. I sign it. *April 2, 2019, Liberty Johansen.*

I make a note to give this to Dad when we finally see him. I make a note to tell him that I understand that he just needed a long walk in the forest because I need those, too, sometimes.

....

Mom looks excited when she walks in the door. She says, "Wow, one of these pairs of boots is great and the other pair is awful! Not even waterproof. What good is that?" She takes off her jacket. "But I may have just found the best sports bra ever."

Jilly giggles at this. I take note to ask Mom what kind of bra it is when it's finally time for me to get a bra. Seems like a useful thing to know.

She asks us how our day was. We both say we're fine. Jilly doesn't mention that she just yelled at Dad and I don't mention that I now talk to a rock.

....

Later, Jilly finally notices the meteorite. We're playing cards on the floor in my room while Mom writes about the things she tested on her hike.

"What's that?" Jilly asks.

I pretend it's no big deal. "A rock."

She crawls over to it and tries to move it. "Why's it so heavy?"

"It's a secret."

"I love secrets," she says.

"It's the meteorite," I say.

She sits and thinks awhile. "From the night the windows broke?"

"Yep."

"You found it?" she asks.

"Yep." She looks at me like I'm a famous explorer and I feel like the older sister again. "You can't tell anybody. Not anybody."

"You know I won't," she says. "Not even Mom."

"Pinkie swears and stick a needle in your eye?"

"That's gross."

"But I mean that big of a promise, right?"

"You found it. Why would anyone want to take it from you? It's just a rock."

"I don't know. People are weird, I guess," I say.

....

Mom calls us downstairs and asks, "How about homemade pizza for dinner?"

Jilly gets excited because she loves Mom's pizza. When Mom asks me what toppings I want on my half, I say, "Whatever you want." Then I go back to my room. I don't really care about dinner or pizza or anything.

"I'm supposed to be getting used to this," I say to the rock.

"Some things are slow," the rock answers.

"I don't understand Dad. He's supposed to be around more. He said he would be. Why'd he lie?"

"I just fell from space. How am I supposed to know?"

"I just fell from space, too," I say. "I guess we're new here."

The rock nods.

"He probably didn't lie on purpose," the rock says.

"How would you know?" I ask.

"I know a lot."

"Are you sure you don't want ham and pineapple?" Mom calls up the steps.

"I'm fine!" I say.

"I'll make ham and pineapple anyway," Mom says.

"As if ham and pineapple will change my life," I say to the rock.

Mom's closer to my door now—just down the attic steps. "You're spending a lot of time in your room this week. Working on star maps?"

"Kinda," I say. "Not really. I don't know." I look at the maps above my bed.

"You should take those down," the rock says.

"I'll never finish them," I say.

"Throw them away," the rock says.

I don't feel like I can throw them away. I made them. Maybe one day I'll figure out the shapes of winter. I've never had this much trouble before. Now it's like every star I drew has the possibility of being part of something else. And at the same time, every star I drew has the possibility of not being part of anything at all.

Just like Dad.

Just like me.

Chapter 16 — The Thing about Leah Jones

You should probably know some more stuff.

About school. And Leah Jones.

Something happened back in January during the week she excommunicated me from the sixth grade.

On my way out of math class that Wednesday Leah said, "I heard your dad left. I can see why."

It had only been five days since Dad moved out. I'd been bracing myself for Leah being mean. It was how she was now.

Everyone knew that.

What everyone didn't know (including me) is that I can be mean right back.

I said, "Happy fake wedding day. I hope Mike knows he's marrying the biggest bitch on the planet."

I didn't know I could do that. I'd never tried. But it felt good. The way eating ice cream feels good. The way a good dream feels good even after you wake up. It felt really, really good.

At lunch no one would let me sit down at our table—excommunicated. So it was my first day sitting with Malik.

Malik ate a ham-and-cheese sandwich with mustard on it. He had mustard on his cheek and didn't know it. It didn't bother me or anything. I've had mustard on my cheek before. "How's school going?" he asked.

"It's good."

"But how's it really going?" he asked. "I mean, you wouldn't be sitting here if it was going really good, you know?" For a fifth grader, Malik is perceptive.

"I was excommunicated from the sixth grade because I said fake weddings at recess were stupid."

Malik has the best laugh. He laughed so hard at that, it made me laugh, too. He even slapped the table and the lunch monitor came over to make sure he wasn't dying from a random peanut. "No one has ever asked me to get pretend-married," Malik said. "I wonder what I'm doing wrong."

"Ugh," I said. "You're doing everything right. Believe me."

"If you want, we can pretend we're married as long as you never eat anything with nuts in it." We laughed.

We ate our lunches for a minute. Malik wiped the mustard from his cheek.

"You still go fishing with your dad?" Malik asked. "Down at that pond you used to tell me about?"

I looked at him and wondered if I should lie. Malik had almost-died three times. I figured he could handle the truth.

"My dad moved out last weekend," I said. "My parents are getting a divorce."

"So no fishing then," he said.

I laughed a little. "Nope. No fishing."

Ms. S. walked over then but I didn't see her. Malik did but he didn't have time to say anything.

"Liberty, would you come with me, please?" I looked down at my half-eaten lunch and she said, "You can bring that and finish it in my office."

I had to admit that I called Leah the B-word. Ms. S. said she was going to call my mom and that I would have to apologize to Leah's face at the end of the day.

I missed recess, which I was happy about. No having to see Leah get fake-married. She'd even worn a white dress, which was stupid because it was January and no one would see the dress under her winter coat anyway.

At the end of the day, ten minutes before the buses lined up outside the school, I looked Leah Jones square in the eye and apologized. I didn't mean a word of it.

....

The next day it was like the whole school was under a weird spell. At the bus stop, Patrick and Finn Nolan didn't even look at Jilly and me. In homeroom, I asked the girl who sat across from me what was wrong, but she gave me a look like asking was inappropriate. Everyone seemed tired. Our math teacher gave us an extra day to get ready for a quiz and let us study in groups. Which meant I studied alone.

At lunch, Malik had a pile of cheese and crackers and a container of grapes. As he started making little cracker sandwiches, I said, "What is wrong with this school today? Everyone is acting weird."

"Don't know," Malik said.

"It's creepy.

Malik said, "Did you hear about Leah's ring?"

"Excommunicated," I said.

"She lost it."

"Who cares about a stupid ring?"

"It was her mom's ring. Real diamonds," Malik said. "They searched all night. Even the teachers stayed late looking for it."

I didn't say anything.

"She's in big trouble at home," Malik said. "Someone told me the ring was worth a million dollars."

I shrugged off the million-dollars thing. Who even knows how much a ring is worth, anyway. But something was wrong with Leah, I knew that. "She keeps staring at me all day," I said. "Maybe she thinks I stole it."

Malik said, "I promise when we finally get married, I won't steal my mom's ring."

Inside of an hour, I was sitting in the chair in front of Ms. S.'s desk again.

"I didn't even see the ring," I said.

"I did tell her mother that you spent recess with me yesterday," she said. "But I wanted to ask just in case."

"I wasn't looking. Sorry," I said. "I think fake weddings are stupid."

Chapter 17 — Nothing Is Fair Nothing Is Fair Nothing Is Fair

Dad still hasn't kept his promise. It's been eighty-four days since we saw him. I don't care now if he needs a long walk in a metaphorical forest. I can't hear his laugh anymore. I can't imagine his eyes anymore. I can't remember anything the way it used to be. And I don't know how to be in this new family. A family of three. A galaxy missing a vital planet. It's like I dreamed all this.

I'm hard. Cold. I'm covered in metallic spots. I'm heavier than myself. I'm the rock. And I want to go back home — to space.

....

Jilly annoyed me all day — right up to when we walked into the house after school. She keeps telling me that I should be nice to Leah Jones so I can get my friends back. Jilly is too young to understand.

"I have to do my homework," I say, and set up at the desk in the living room.

She says, "I'm going out to swing." She says it like I should be proud of her or something. For doing what normal kids do. Whatever. She can be normal all she wants.

Mom is making spaghetti and meatballs for dinner. I'm not hungry. I decide to skip my homework and I go upstairs and lie on my bed. The unfinished star maps on my ceiling mock me.

Your idea to change the world is stupid.

You'll never be anyone important.

I stand up and rip them off the slanted ceiling. I throw them on the floor and sit back down on my bed. I curse a few times under my breath. I'm probably a monster.

"You're not a monster," the rock says.

"You can't even talk," I say.

"Okay. You're *probably* not a monster," it says.

"Why's everything so unfair?"

"Nothing is fair," the rock says.

"Nothing is fair," I say.

"Are you sure you don't know anything about Leah's ring?" the rock asks.

"Of course not," I say.

The rock doesn't say anything.

"Why'd you even ask that?" I say.

The rock doesn't say anything.

"None of this is fair," I say.

I go back downstairs. The spaghetti is on the stove and Jilly is back inside and she and Mom are playing twenty questions. Jilly always picks really weird animals. Mom and I can never guess them. Unfair. This is my life.

I set the table and don't play along.

By the time we sit down, Jilly tells Mom her animal was a star-nosed mole. Mom acts like it's cool that Jilly tricked us. I roll my eyes.

"What?" Jilly asks.

"Nothing."

"Why'd you roll your eyes and breathe like that?" she asks.

"I didn't," I say. But I did.

"Yes you did," she says.

"Whatever."

Mom sits down after dishing out spaghetti and meatballs onto plates.

"It hurts my feelings," Jilly says.

"I didn't do anything," I say.

"You rolled your eyes!"

"Star-nosed mole? Like we'd ever even know that," I say.

"So you did roll your eyes!" Jilly says.

I'm less hungry than I was when I first sat down. I look at my plate and I can't figure out how I'm going to eat this much food.

"It's unfair," I say.

"Because I know more than you?" Jilly says.

My face gets hot. Like I'm sick or something. I can't get a deep breath.

"Eat your dinner," Mom says to both of us.

I try to eat. Small mouthfuls. But I'm too hot to chew.

"You're just mad because nobody at school likes you," Jilly says.

"That's rude," Mom says. "Be nice to your sister."

"I'll be nice to her if she's nice to me," Jilly says.

"I was nice to you. Every single day of your life," I say.

"You weren't nice just now," Jilly says.

"You picked a stupid animal. Your choice. And that's not nice, either," I say.

"It's a game!" she says.

"Star-nosed mole? It's not a very fun game if we don't even know what you're talking about," I say.

"You're a mean sister," Jilly yells.

"I walked you to homeroom for the last two months," I say.

She's crying. I'm not. This shows that I'm mature and she isn't. I can own my mistakes and she can't. Ask any star-nosed mole. I bet *they* even know that they're weird and no one has heard of them.

"Liberty, stop making your sister cry," Mom says.

I look at my plate of food.

My face gets so hot I can't hold my fork, so I drop it. It lands on the floor.

The sound of the fork hitting the floor makes me jump. I look left.

"I'M SICK OF ALL THIS YELLING!" I say. I yell. I say-yell in a voice I've never heard before.

I close my eyes, tilt back my head, and make this sound: "OOOOOOEEEEEAAAHHHYYYY."

Mom and Jilly don't say anything at first. I can't see them because my eyes are closed. Then they say a bunch of stuff but I don't listen to it. Jilly's still crying. Everything is unfair.

"I AM ASKING YOU ALL TO BE QUIET SO I CAN JUST THINK FOR A MINUTE!" I say. "GGGGGRRRR RRAAAAAAAAAAEEEEEEOOOO!"

I go on a sort of journey in my head. I run away and live in the woods. I run away and become Amish. I run away and find my spaceship and finally go home. I stop at Finn Nolan's house and take him with me because I worry about him even though I shouldn't. It's not like he's worried about me. Nothing is fair.

I open my eyes, but it's like I've been away for three months. I expect to see everyone here, eating dinner like normal.

Mom and Jilly look startled. Dad still isn't here.

"AHHHOOOOOAAAHHOOOO!" I yell.

I get up from the table and pace around the kitchen. I step on my fork and I curse because it hurts.

Mom says some stuff but I can't understand it.

I close my eyes and inside my eyelids, I can see the night sky. At least two thousand stars.

"I HATE EVERYONE ON EARTH AND WISH I COULD GO BACK TO MY PLANET!" I say.

I do a jumping jack and shake my head. I feel dizzy.

"BBBBBBRRRRROOOOOOOOOYYYYYYEEEEEE!"

My ears ring and I think I may be louder than the loudest thing on Earth.

"WHY ARE YOU LOOKING AT ME LIKE THAT?" I say.

Jilly is now sitting on Mom's lap. I don't know how she got there. They look so happy without me. Just the two of them. I should probably move in with Dad. Nothing is fair.

"STOP LOOKING AT ME LIKE THAT!" I say.

They keep looking at me. There's sweat on my face, I'm so hot.

"AAAAAAAAARRRRRRRHHHHHHHHH!"

I pick up the toaster.

I'm not sure why, exactly, I pick up the toaster.

It's just there.

Mom and Jilly are still sitting together, Jilly's arms wrapped around Mom's neck. Mom is saying something to me—I can see her mouth moving but I can't hear any words.

I throw the toaster at the window.

The toaster goes through the window.

I thought it would bounce off. I know it's a window and it's made of glass, but I really thought the toaster would bounce off and land on the kitchen floor. Instead it goes through.

Another broken window.

Another reason for Lou to come into our house and show us that we need a man.

Another time I make Mom feel bad because she didn't mean for this to happen. She was just doing what anyone else would do in her situation but I don't know what her situation is because she can't tell me.

"I NEED TO HAVE A BATH!" I yell.

I run up the stairs to the bathroom and turn on the water.

I look at myself in the mirror and I look like myself except I wish I looked like someone else. I wish I *was* someone else. I wish I knew what a star-nosed mole was. I wish I knew why I threw the toaster. I wish I didn't have any family. I wish I was the rock.

Rocks don't know the difference between unfair and fair.

Rocks don't need parents. Or sisters.

Rocks can't be excommunicated from the sixth grade.

Nobody wants to marry a rock at recess.

....

Mom checks in on me in the bath which is awkward but I get it. She's making sure I'm okay. Not throwing toasters. Not cursing. Not yelling weird sounds that don't make any sense. I wave at her and she smiles and then closes the door again. I go back to looking at the stars inside my eyelids. My ears are underwater and I'm communicating with my people.

I have the tiny meteorite. I'm tapping on the bathtub with it. I'm making a rhythm. It's the rhythm of space. It's like Morse code but better because no one can decode it but me and the stars.

H—E—L—P—M—E.

The stars send me a message inside my brain: *There was no meteorite. I am the meteorite. I fell from space, endured impossible atmosphere. Crabby professor would say I'm not a meteorite. I bet crabby professor doesn't like to be wrong about things. But he is. I'm a meteorite.*

Except I'm a girl, too.

....

The meteorite is still in my bedroom, proof that it's the meteorite, not me. But I'm in my bedroom too so maybe we can both be the meteorite. We both fell from space. We both got really hot and made a loud noise and broke the windows in Lou's log cabin.

"Sometimes I wish I was an alien," I say when I come down from my bath.

Mom nods. She pauses a video that she's showing Jilly on the computer.

Jilly says, "I think you probably are one."

"What would be cool about being an alien?" Mom asks.

"Everything," I say. "I'd know about space travel and other species and I'd see humans as an inferior race and not want to, like, fit in with them or anything." Mom and Jilly look at me with sad eyes. "And I could just take off whenever I want. In my spaceship. Back to wherever I came from."

"I'd miss you," Jilly says.

"You could come with me!"

"It would be so cool to see Earth from space," Mom says. "Can you imagine?"

I've seen pictures like anyone else has. But no, I can't imagine what it would be like to see Earth from space because if I got off this planet, I wouldn't look back. Even if I landed somewhere that smelled like farts all the time. Even if I landed on a planet that's dark all the time. Or light. Or cold. Or hot. Or even if I landed on a planet that had yodeling music playing twenty-four hours a day, I wouldn't look back.

Chapter 18 — Hot Dogs Are Okay Now

SUNDAY, APRIL 14, 2019

Sunday morning. Mom comes downstairs, gets a cup of coffee, and says, "Dad's going to take you guys for a while today." She says this as if it's something we've done before.

"Like last weekend?" Jilly asks. "And the one before that?"

Jilly's sarcasm is really coming along.

"For real. He's coming at around eleven," Mom says.

I bet she talked him into it because of the toaster thing.

I haven't been myself.

....

Dad picks us up at our house and it's weird. Like, the-light-during-an-eclipse weird. It feels like a dream.

First, he's skinny. Too skinny. Like I-could-see-in-Jilly's-eyes-that-she's-afraid-he's-sick skinny.

Second, he parks in the driveway and waits until we come outside. As if Mom isn't here at all. It's as if he thinks Jilly and I have been living in the cabin on our own for the last eighty-six days.

Third, he's wearing a baseball cap. Dad never owned a baseball cap when I knew him. He looks like someone else's dad.

We get in the car and drive down the lane.

"We're gonna see some stars tonight," he says.

"I have school tomorrow," I say.

"Since when does that matter?" he asks.

Jilly says, "I'm right here, you know. I don't like stars."

We're both in the back seat and Jilly scowls at me and I roll my eyes at her like Dad is being weird because he *is* being weird and I have nothing to do with it. Jilly makes a funny face and it makes me smile. I reach over and hold her hand. She leans into my ear and says, "He smells weird."

Add to my list: Fourth, Dad is wearing cologne and that's weirder than all the other stuff I've listed already.

"How about a baseball game?" Dad says.

Jilly and I don't answer because we don't really watch baseball because we don't have a TV that's connected to cable channels. Also, Finn Nolan and Ethan McGarret are on the baseball team and I'm pretty sure I don't care about baseball at all.

"Or we could go over to my place first?" he asks.

"Whatever you want to do," I say.

"I wanna see your apartment!" Jilly says.

So we go to his apartment on Porter Drive. Which is more like a town house than an apartment. It's modern, two stories, and has wall-to-wall carpet. Big new TV. Our old fish tank, but with new fish. Not much furniture. Nothing on the walls. It looks like he still thinks it's temporary.

"Where's our room?" Jilly asks.

"That one," he points.

"But . . . where are the bunk beds?" Jilly asks.

"Oh. I. Uh. They're coming soon," Dad says.

"You've been gone for three months and you didn't get the bunk beds yet?" I ask.

"I've been doing other stuff," Dad says.

"Like not eating from the looks of things," Jilly says.

Dad wants to say something. Instead he takes a deep breath through his nose and lets it out through his mouth and smiles kinda pained.

"Okay," Jilly says. "I'm good with leaving any time you want."

I look in the kitchen. There are dishes piled in the sink and three glasses next to it. One glass has a lipstick mark on it. I run it under the tap and wash off the lipstick so Jilly won't see. "Me too," I say.

We go to a baseball game. Dad had tickets all along and I guess he didn't want to force us to go, but he seems happy once we're in the stands and watching the game. He buys us hot dogs and I try not to think of all the things he used to say about how hot dogs are bad for us. I'm just glad to see him eat something.

By the sixth inning, Jilly is bored and I'm thinking about lipstick. Mom doesn't wear lipstick. That's what I'm thinking.

"I want to go home," Jilly says in my ear.

"I know."

"Like right now. I have to go home." She looks terrified, like she's having some sort of anxiety attack.

I pull her into my side and hug her. "Dad," I say. "Can we go now?"

"We're not even to the seventh-inning stretch!"

I give him a look like we really have to go now, so we get up and make our way down the bleachers and to the parking lot.

In the car, he says, "I feel like we're strangers."

I say, "Don't worry. It'll get easier."

"Maybe if you wouldn't have ignored us since January," Jilly says. Or half says. I can hear her because I'm in the back seat with her, but I don't know if Dad can hear her.

He doesn't say anything else.

I think he heard her.

....

We end up at the diner in our little town's Main Street. Everyone looks at the three of us as they come in and pick up their take-out food or wait to get seated. I feel pity from every single person. It's like we have a cloud above our booth that says *DIVORCE* in cuddly, puffy black letters.

"It was great to finally see you guys," Dad says.

Jilly doesn't say anything.

I say, "It's good to see you, too."

"I miss you so much," he says.

Jilly doesn't say anything.

I say, "We miss you, too."

Fact is, I still miss him now, right here, in the diner. He's not doing any Dad things. He looks distracted.

When he drops us off at the cabin, he doesn't get out of the car. He offers us hugs over the back of his seat like he's dropping us off to school in the morning. I lean in and give him a squeeze and say, "I love you." Jilly just gets out of her side of the car, closes the door, and goes inside.

"Do you think she'll be okay?" he asks me.

"She's doing better than you think."

"Seems really angry to me," he says.

"So?"

"So I hope she's not like that next time," he says.

"If next time is three more months, then she probably will be," I say.

"I—"

"Eat more food. You look too skinny," I say. We meet eyes. His eyes look hurt. I blink twice, force a smile, close the car door, and go inside.

Jilly is crying in her room and Mom is downstairs in the kitchen scrubbing the sink. She just scrubbed it a few days ago, so if I was to guess, she's trying to scrub all the way through to Australia to not be here in the cabin. To not be here in a divorce. To not be here in a Sunday when her daughters went to a baseball game with a stranger.

Chapter 19 — Me and Jan's Whiteboard

I knew I would eventually end up in here. Leah Jones. Toaster. Talking to a rock.

"How are things with Liberty?" Jan asks.

"It's going okay," I say.

We smile at each other.

"I heard you got pretty mad last week," she says.

"I'm probably mad all the time. I don't know."

"You've had a hard year," she says. "How's school?"

I shrug. I don't really want to tell her about Leah Jones. If I do, it looks like I think the same way Leah Jones thinks and I don't. "Jilly seems to be doing better," I say.

She's quiet for a minute. Then she asks, "Want to tell me what you have against toasters?"

I laugh. I'm not sure why. "It was the first thing I saw." She nods.

"It was like I didn't have control of my arms. Or my mouth. Or anything," I say.

"What were you thinking when you threw it?" she asks.

"I wasn't thinking anything. It was just — I was just — really mad. Like, sometimes I want to go back to wherever I'm from. Mars or wherever. You know? I mean, life would be easier and maybe I'd make friends there."

"Wouldn't your friends on Earth miss you?"

"I don't have any friends on Earth," I say.

"I'm sure you have somebody," she says.

"Trust me. I don't have one friend." I feel bad because I have Malik, but I only have him at lunch, so it's not like I'm lying. "I used to have Finn, because he lives down the road, and for a while I was best friends with Leah. But now I'm a freak because Dad moved out."

"Wow," she says.

"I don't miss them. They're all immature and think about boyfriends and girlfriends all the time."

"Oh. I can understand why that's annoying," Jan says. "But why no friends?"

"I'm just afraid if I talk to anyone, people will tell Leah."

"Who's Leah?"

"She's the girl who excommunicated me from the sixth grade class."

"Excommunicated?" she asks.

I nod.

"Does she have the power to do that?" Jan asks. She asks me to explain why Leah has so much power and I do. It all sounds stupid. Other girls want to be Leah. Boys want to marry Leah. Teachers think she's great because she gets good grades and does exactly what they want her to do. Also, she has all the right clothes.

"She sounds kinda boring," Jan says.

"She is boring," I say.

"So why'd she excommunicate you from the sixth grade?" Jan asks. "And what about the boy down the road?"

"Finn Nolan. I really don't want to talk about it," I say. "I want to talk about Dad."

She nods.

"He was so weird on Sunday," I say.

She nods.

"Like maybe that's why he wasn't happy when he lived with us—maybe he just wanted to take a long quiet walk in the forest without me. Or Jilly." I almost cry a little. "Like—maybe we're the problem."

Jan shakes her head. "Having a parent struggling with depression is hard," she says. "Trust me. Feeling like this is normal. But you're not the problem."

I say, "I guess."

"Your mom says you and your dad were into the stars, too. That you used to draw maps of stars together or something like that."

I don't say anything.

Jan looks at the whiteboard on her wall. She says, "Draw me something."

I get up from the chair and uncap a blue marker. I draw the North Star in the middle of the board, mark N, S, E, & W, and start filling in from there. Bigger dots for bigger stars. Smaller dots for smaller stars.

"Wow," Jan says. "That's pretty cool. I didn't know you could do that."

"How would you know?" I ask as I keep drawing.

"I don't know. I thought maybe your mom or your sister would have explained."

"Jilly and Mom are having a really hard time," I say.

"What about you?" she asks.

"I'm okay," I say.

"But you're throwing the toaster around. Does that seem okay?"

"I have to help them adjust," I say. I'm filling in smaller stars now. I don't want to turn around and look at Jan. I feel like I'm going to cry.

"Help who adjust?" she asks.

"Jilly and Mom. And Dad, when I see him. He's skinny. Too skinny. And Mom never gets to do anything because he keeps canceling and she's probably dying to go hiking with her friends," I say.

"And how are you helping Jilly?"

"I play games with her every day and walk her to home-room and protect her on the bus from the Nolan brothers and hug her when she cries."

"Who hugs you when you cry?" she asks.

"I don't cry," I say.

"Why not?"

"I'm fine."

"Okay," she says. She waits a few seconds. I finally sit back down in the chair and I look over at the white-board. Jan's looking at it, too. "Can I tell you what I think?"

I nod.

"I think you're putting everyone before Liberty. I think you're a really helpful girl and you were probably already putting your family before yourself long before your dad moved out. I think you can't see this because you're so used to it," she says.

"Please stop calling me Liberty. I'm sitting right here," I say.

"Sorry," she says. "But do you see what I mean? Because you've lived with parental depression your whole life, you've probably been doing *this* your whole life. Does that make sense?"

"I guess." We never really talk about Dad's depression, so this is weird.

Jan says that maybe I'm hiding my feelings. She says maybe I'm scared to peek out from my shell—like a turtle. I don't say anything. I don't think I'm a turtle. I think I'm pretty good at showing my feelings. I got here by throwing a toaster, anyway.

She says, "I have homework for you. Nothing big, but it can be hard."

"Okay."

"I want you to let people in your life deal with their own messes. If your sister is sad, let her be sad and don't try to make her happy."

"That's mean," I say.

"How will she learn to make herself happy if you're always doing it for her?"

"I—" I stop myself because I have no idea how to answer her question.

"Let them be them. You be you. Promise me that you'll think about it," she says. She looks over at the whiteboard. "Is that the Big Dipper?"

"Yep," I say.

"It's accurate?" she asks.

"Did you think I just put dots up there without knowing what they were?"

She shakes her head like she can't believe it. "I'm concerned about what's going on at school. Have you told your mom? Does she know about this Leah girl and how no one talks to you?"

"She knows a little bit."

"I think you should tell her everything. She can talk to the principal," she says.

"I'll talk to her," I say, but I don't mean it. Next year is middle school. More kids from the other elementary schools and I'm sure I'll find a friend.

....

That night, I can't sleep right. I keep thinking about Leah Jones and Mom telling the principal. I can't tell Ms. S. what's going on. It just wouldn't be right.

Anyway, things at school are a little better than January. Some people in my class are even trying to talk to me again. I bet they'd let me sit at the cafeteria table, but I still eat lunch with Malik. He's the only one I trust.

Leah's missing ring story has died down. No one ever

found it and Leah's mom must have figured out how to be okay with that. People have to be okay with all kinds of things.

Missing rings, missing fathers.

Things go missing all the time.

Except I know where Dad is.

And I know where the ring is, too.

Part Three:

SO

NOW

YOU

THINK

I'M A THIEF

Chapter 20 — Countdown

Jilly has started her countdown to the last day of school on the chalkboard in the kitchen.

"Forty-two days left!" she says.

School ends on June 14 this year.

The whole month of April, we didn't go camping once. Which is weird because that's when we'd usually start. Mom was still testing out the boots and other gear she got from work by walking around Lou's fifty acres and pitching tents and stringing flysheets in the backyard. Wasn't the same. One day I came home and she had three sleeping bags in the living room. She said we were going to pretend-camp.

Definitely wasn't the same.

Now it's May. Forty-two days until the last day of school. One hundred and five days since the beginning of our fall from space.

And now you think I'm a thief.

But I didn't steal anything.

Misplacing and stealing are two different things.

....

We were supposed to stay with Dad this weekend—we haven't seen him since the baseball game three weeks ago. It was supposed to be our first official all-weekend stay in the new bunk beds, but he called Mom five minutes ago to tell her he can't do it. Again.

Mom was supposed to go hiking with her friends. Her pack was by the back door ready to go—next to our backpacks. When she hung up with Dad, she slung all three packs onto her back, dropped ours in our rooms, and went to her room to unpack hers.

"You okay?" I ask when she comes downstairs.

"Fine. How are you two?"

Jilly gives a thumbs-up and I say, "Good." Her face looks concerned. I add, "Are you sure you're okay?"

"Totally fine," she says. "But I want to get outside. How about we go to the hill together tonight?"

"I don't know," I say. "I don't really feel like it."

"You could make a map!" she says. With an exclamation point. As if that's exciting.

Once Jilly is in bed and snoring, we go to the hill.

Mom likes to just lie here and stare. I do too. I have paper in front of me and a pencil in my hand, but I don't want to draw. I want to tell Mom about Leah, mostly, but I don't know how to bring it up.

"What's that one?" Mom asks.

I look toward where she's pointing. "What's it look like to you?"

"A giraffe."

"Then it's a giraffe," I say.

"Isn't there already a giraffe up here?"

"Yours looks more like a giraffe than that one."

"What's the bright star on his head?" she asks.

"Arcturus."

"It's amazing that you know all this at your age."

"I was raised by you," I say.

"Your dad gave you the stars, Lib. That's his thing."

Silence.

"He's been so weird," I say. "Especially when he took us to the baseball game."

"Yeah, well, he's just getting used to life on his own, I guess," she says.

I look at Mom's giraffe stars, Arcturus brighter than the others. "So how come he couldn't take us this weekend?" The stars turn into a wineglass—the kind with the long stem. Around the top is a lipstick stain. I don't draw any of it.

"That's adult-stuff," she says.

My limbs go tingly and numb at the same time. I want to say something but I don't know what to say. I stay quiet because maybe Mom will eventually realize that her answer was insulting.

I look back at the sky. I see three new constellations.

An explosion.

A broom.

A frying pan—the frying pan I learned to make grilled cheese sandwiches in that's at Dad's house now.

I sit up and hurry to get the dots on the paper. I connect them. I see that the explosion is in front of the broom, as if the broom is cleaning up a mess. And the frying pan acts as the dustpan—the place where the broom is collecting the explosion.

Mom says, "Are you all right?"

I hum and nod. No time to answer her. No time to explain how it feels to get the pictures before I draw. No time to clean up another mess of insulting answers and excuses. No time to tell her about Leah Jones and the missing ring.

When I turn off my headlamp and lie back down on the blanket, I see it clearly in the sky. I am the broom. I am the explosion. I am the frying pan.

Chapter 21 — Gravity-Bound Broom

Jilly is petting the meteorite like it's a cat.

"I don't get it," Jilly says. "I know Dad loves us but he doesn't seem it."

"He loves us," I say. "But he's just going through something hard, I guess."

We're on my bedroom floor doing a jigsaw puzzle that we'll never finish.

"I'm going through something hard too," she says. "Doesn't mean I just throw my family away."

"Yeah. I know."

"I hate this puzzle," she says.

"Me too. Let's put it away and do something else."

The phone rings. Both of us sit up straighter.

Mom tries to keep her voice down, but she can't. House is too small and her feelings are too big. "You can't just waltz in halfway through Sunday," she says. "I'm already making dinner."

Mom isn't making dinner but I don't care that she's lying.

"No. Not while you're like this," she says. "No. Not even on speakerphone."

Jilly hears this and can't stop herself and I'm not fast enough to stop her either. She runs down the stairs and says, "I want to talk to him!"

It wasn't supposed to be like this. That's what Mom will say later.

....

People think depression looks like one thing. Sadness, usually. I guess people who don't know much about depression think that people who have it walk around crying or being pessimistic all the time. But depression isn't that easy to describe. It's different for everybody. From what Dad's said, he feels like someone else, which is weird, but since I've known him for twelve years, I can say that it looks that way from the outside, too.

It makes him do things like snap or yell or stare into space or drive away for a few hours or sit in a room with no lights on for a day or hug us too long or curse and say he shouldn't be on planet Earth. It makes him do things like cancel our weekend together on a Friday and then call up on a Sunday and ask Mom if he can have us for a few hours because he feels delayed-bad for canceling.

"Hey there, kiddo!" I hear his pixelated speakerphone voice echo in the kitchen.

"So whatcha doing?" Jilly asks.

"Well, I called Mom to ask if maybe I could take you girls out to dinner tonight but she . . . uh . . . but it might not be a good idea. So we'll have to save it for our next weekend together."

"When's that?"

"I don't know," he says.

Mom says, "It's the seventeenth."

"It's forty days 'til the end of school," Jilly says.

Dad says, "Hold on. It can't be the seventeenth. I have plans."

Mom doesn't say anything and I feel like I should go downstairs but I know if I do, my arms will turn into brooms and I will try to clean up the mess that's being made over the phone line.

"It's forty days until the last day of school," Jilly says again.

"We're going to have to switch out weekends," Dad says. "I'm not here on the seventeenth."

Mom says, "Jack, you've had the schedule for months. It's on your phone calendar. It's in a spreadsheet. It's what you agreed to. You can't just switch things in and out."

"And Liberty found a meteorite!" Jilly says. My heart drops.

Dad laughs. "It's probably not a meteorite, honey. Those are pretty rare."

"How would you know?" Jilly says. "You haven't even seen it." I hear her walking and then stomping up the steps. My arms are brooms. My legs are brooms.

All I hear before Jilly explodes into my room is Mom saying, "You can pick the girls up on the seventeenth at five, like it says on the paperwork . . . No . . . No. Stop, Jack. Just . . . I'll talk to you when you're feeling better."

"Can you believe he said that?" Jilly says.

"Yeah. He's not himself," I say.

"He's a jerk is what he is," Jilly says.

"Don't say that."

"It's true."

"He can act like a jerk sometimes, but he's not a jerk," I say with my broom mouth, my broom tongue.

"What's wrong with you?" Jilly says. "Why aren't you mad? It's your meteorite!"

"We had a deal," I say.

"I know . . . but I wanted to tell him. You know, so maybe he'd come get us when he's supposed to or something. I mean, it's a meteorite, right? It's something he's interested in. It's . . . it's special." At this, Jilly crumbles.

All my brain can come up with to say are broom words. *You're special. You're more special than a meteorite. You're interesting. He didn't mean it that way. He's unwell.*

Instead I say, "I can't believe you told him. Just leave me alone."

Before I can find my broom hands to clean up my own mess, I'm walking down the stairs, through the kitchen, past Mom, who's staring into space at the kitchen table, and out the back door. Across the deck. Across the yard. Down the path that leads to Lou's first tree stand. Mosquitoes are out. They bite me and get bellies-full of broom blood. I don't even swat them away or turn back for bug spray.

I get to the tree stand—a metal platform high in a tree with a ladder—and I climb. Hunters sit up here for hours in the fall waiting for deer to walk into range. I lie on the platform and I feel weightless. Then I roll on my side and look out over the forest and scare myself thinking about how far I would fall if I fell.

....

When I go back inside, Mom has dinner almost ready. I set the table and we sit down to eat.

Jilly starts crying before we even start eating. "I'm sorry, okay?"

I nod and force out a smile so she won't make a big deal.

Mom says, "What's going on?"

Jilly says, "Nothing," through her tears. It's not convincing. Obviously.

I eat the rest of my dinner in silence.

When I'm done loading the dishwasher, I take my Sunday-night shower.

I see myself as the broom. I watch as all the dirt I swept up spirals down the drain. It's a lot of dirt. More than just today. More than a month. More than a few months—since the week we fell, or before that.

I think about how maybe I was a broom before I ever knew it.

I talk to the rock about it.

"Jan was right," I say.

The rock says, "You should probably tell your mom about Leah and the ring."

"Don't change the subject."

"I'm right, though," the rock says.

"I'm not even talking about that," I say. "I'm talking about how I clean up everyone's messes."

"Okay," the rock says.

"It's not about any of that other stuff," I say.

"Okay," the rock says.

Don't think I'm going irrational. It's just that I need a friend and what better friend to have than one that's been in space? How many kids at my school have been to space? None. How many of my parents? None. How many psychologists? None.

Chapter 22 — The Library Holds My Secret

Library day at school starts with a jinx.

At the bus stop, Finn Nolan asks me if I did my science homework.

"Yeah," I say.

"Can I borrow it?" he asks. "Just for the ride to school."

I don't want to say yes. But I also know Finn needs the homework. But I also know he could toss it out the window just to get me in trouble.

I hand it to him and he says, "Thanks, Liberty. You're saving my butt."

He gave me the paper back when we got off the bus and said thanks again.

I just never know what I'm getting with Finn Nolan.

Library is the second class of the day. I hover by the *R* books in the fiction section. I pretend like I'm looking for a book, but I'm not. I'm looking at the place I hid Leah Jones's ring. I'm wondering what I should do about it.

Leah is sitting at a study desk with her fake-husband of four months, Mike, and they're giggling about something. She looks at me and I look away. She says, "Mrs. Hanson! Liberty is staring at me again!"

The librarian ignores her. Or doesn't hear her.

I start sweating. I try to take a few deep breaths. It's as if the air-conditioning in the whole building just got switched off.

"Liberty? Come sit down. You're red. And pale."

In my mind I'm thinking no one can be red and pale at the same time, but I feel both red and pale, and Mrs. Hanson is a librarian, so she probably knows best.

I keep my eyes closed once I sit at her chair. The room rises in a buzz of conversation as she kneels next to me and asks if I can make it to the nurse's office.

"I probably just need some air," I say.

She touches my forehead. "You're burning up."

Just like a meteor hitting the atmosphere.

The nurse takes my temperature and I'm 102.3. I fall asleep on the cot waiting for Mom to pick me up.

Three hours later I'm taking a pill the size of a small dog. It's strep throat. I have to stay home for the rest of the week, but I should be fine for our weekend with Dad. Mom works from home on Thursday and Friday because she's worried. On Friday she finds me standing in the kitchen staring at the toaster.

"You okay?" she asks.

"Yeah. Fine."

I can't tell her what's really happening.

Every time I walk by the toaster, I still feel like throwing it.

Every time I walk by the *R* bookshelf in the school library, I want to retrieve Leah's mom's ring and return it.

I don't do either.

Chapter 23 — Snooping Can Really Ruin Breakfast

First sleepover at Dad's house. The bunk beds are great. The kitchen is filled with our favorite snacks. Jilly seems fine and I'm okay.

Dad is still skinny and kind of pale. He says he's sorry this took so long. He wants Jilly and me to know he's getting better but he doesn't know how to tell us because he says he's not good at talking. We're in the kitchen.

"It's like there's a thing that makes me mad when I'm not even mad. But I am mad, just not at you. Or your mom. I'm mad at stuff that has nothing to do with you guys. At all."

Jilly and I look at each other.

He says, "I know you've heard me yelling but it wasn't really me yelling."

It was totally him yelling, by the way. No one else came into the house and yelled for him.

"I mean, of course it was me yelling. And you heard me yelling at your mom but she didn't do anything wrong. Same as when I yelled at you two. You didn't do anything wrong. It's me, not you. You know? I mean, I have problems."

Jilly and I are nodding now. We're hoping this ends soon. I don't even remember him yelling much, really. Not at me and Jilly anyway.

"I'm so sorry for everything I've caused. I mean everything I did and stuff. You didn't deserve that and you deserved a good dad and I couldn't always be that good dad and I just want to say I'm sorry."

I know it's hard to keep up. I know he seems like a bad guy but he's not.

Dad is a planet spiraling out of orbit, pretending to be perfectly in orbit.

"But how is it really, Dad? Like—how are you *now*?" I ask. I am gravity. Planets can't just wander off and think everything is fine with the rest of the galaxy.

"Well, I don't know. I miss you guys. I miss coming home to you. I missed going camping with you in April. And I miss tucking you in at night. I don't know."

Jilly and I sit and stare at him.

"Who wants Oreos?" he says, and gets up from the couch and goes into the kitchen. "Anyone up for an episode of *Star Trek*?"

"It's four o'clock," Jilly says. "We haven't eaten dinner yet."

"So?"

"So we should eat dinner and *then* eat Oreos," she says.

"Sounds like your mom talking," he says.

Jilly looks hurt.

I say, "I think we should wait until after dinner. For the cookies and the *Star Trek*."

"Suit yourselves," he says, and then proceeds to eat three Oreos right in front of us.

Dad isn't getting any better at this. Also, since when does he eat Oreos?

....

We eat dinner at the diner in town and I get a grilled cheese sandwich because no matter where I go, that's what I eat. Dad tries to get me to try other things, but I ignore him until the waitress comes and I tell her I want a grilled cheese sandwich. He makes a disapproving grunt and concentrates on Jilly.

The more I watch the two of them giggling and being goofy, the more I wonder about which one of us is more like Dad. Sometimes I am — stars, knots, and fishing — and sometimes Jilly is with her temper, goofy side, and how she's always crying over stuff. This leads me to thinking that maybe one day Jilly could get depression.

I know the kinds of things Dad said to Mom before he finally left. I don't know if I could handle if Jilly thought those things about herself. I love her too much. I love her so much I want her to stop holding Dad's hand on the diner's table. I want her to stop making him feel happy while we're here because deep down he's not happy and this is fake and I don't understand why he can't just admit that he's not happy. It's as obvious as my grilled cheese sandwich.

Before we go to sleep, Jilly says from the bottom bunk, "He seems to be doing okay."

"Yeah."

"He still smells weird, though," she says.

....

I still have to take the dog-sized pills for strep throat and Dad decides to put whipped cream on Saturday morning to make it go down easier. This is the Dad I miss. Not awake enough to have even thought about this—just saw the whipped cream and the pill I'd left on the counter and he did it because it's funny. And now he's disco dancing to some funky music on the radio while he squeezes fresh orange juice and sings off-tune. I watch him from the living room. This is Dad. The Dad I miss. The Dad I want back. I almost forgot about him.

"You feeling better?" he asks.

"My throat doesn't hurt anymore, so that's good."

"You didn't bring me any star maps," he says. "Maybe we can go out tonight and do one?"

"I'll see how I'm feeling," I say. "Doctor told me to take it easy."

"Okay," he says. Then he yells so Jilly can hear him. "What do you guys want for breakfast?"

"Bacon!" Jilly yells from upstairs.

He looks at me and bends down an eyebrow. "Since when does she like bacon?"

I shrug.

"I don't have bacon!" he yells to Jilly. "But I can make you a ham, egg, and cheese sandwich!"

"Yay!" Jilly says.

"Dad, I worry about you," I say. "I just want you to be okay." He stops digging in the fridge and looks at me. Opens his arms for a hug. I fall into them.

He really hugs me, too. No pats on the back or quick release. He still smells like the perfume counter at the mall.

"You shouldn't worry."

I wait for him to say more but he doesn't. We break the hug and he holds me by my shoulders and smiles. It's not a picture smile or a happy smile. It's the kind of smile he gave me when a fish in our old tank used to die and I'd cry because he was going to flush it down the toilet instead of giving it a proper memorial.

I shouldn't worry. But that makes me worry more. About him. About me.

"You got a new bed!" Jilly says when she comes into the kitchen.

Dad nods.

"Why'd you get a new bed?" she asks.

"Got tired of the old one. Hurt my back."

"But it's so big!"

I watch Dad and I know he's lying. I'm not sure why he's lying, but he does this thing when he lies. He keeps things short and changes the subject.

"Liberty, do you feel good enough for a short hike maybe?"

Like that.

"Let's go to Hawk Mountain!" Jilly says.

"I could probably do Hawk Mountain," I answer.

Dad starts making egg, ham, and cheese sandwiches for the three of us and I go up the steps to see his new bed. Jilly was right. It's huge. I don't understand why he'd need such a huge bed.

I'm not dumb. I'm twelve. I know what happens in grown-ups' beds other than sleeping. I mean, I kinda know. I don't get the details but I know enough.

I don't know what's wrong with me, but I walk right over to the side of the bed where Dad sleeps—you can tell by which side the clock is on and two books—and I open the drawer of his nightstand. I know this makes me a snooper.

The minute I see what's in the drawer, I close the drawer. I feel strep throat heat all over my body and I go into Jilly's and my room and sit on her bottom bunk.

Breathe in. Breathe out.

I make a list in my head of the things I'm glad I *didn't* find in the drawer. A dragon, a hunk of old cheese, an alligator. Nope. I can't make the list.

I wish I'd never become a snooper. Snoopers can't unsee what they see. And I can't unknow that Dad isn't the only person sleeping in his big, new bed.

My brain wants to know if it was her lipstick on the glass I saw the first time I was here. My brain wants to know if this is why Dad left. My brain wants to know if this is why Dad keeps canceling our weekends together.

My brain wants to storm downstairs and ask him everything.

And as it so happens, my brain controls my nerves, which send messages to my muscles, and the next thing I know, I'm in the kitchen and Dad is just putting a plate out for me.

"Breakfast is served!" he says.

I say, "Who is she?"

Chapter 24 – Dad's House Has Cable TV

Dad looks a mix of shocked and angry.

"You got a big bed. You have new clothes," I say.

Jilly says, "And you smell weird."

"Eat your breakfast," Dad says. He glances at Jilly, then back to me.

"Jilly's old enough to know," I say.

"Know what?" she asks. Which means she's not old enough to know.

"Eat your breakfast," he says again. "You'll need your strength to get up to the North Lookout. We might even see an eagle."

More lies. Because now we're talking about eagles.

"I don't feel good," I say. "Not sure if I can make it."

Jilly pouts. "You felt fine a minute ago."

"I'm hot and I feel like I probably shouldn't do too much," I say.

We eat our breakfast quiet as a walk in the forest.

Jilly goes upstairs to the bathroom after breakfast.

"Look," Dad says to me. "We've had this conversation before. No snooping in my stuff."

"I didn't snoop. I just saw the huge bed and noticed you smell different and you have new clothes."

"It's for my job."

"You have to smell nice for your job?" Dad works at the same place he's worked since I can remember. Smelling nice was never important before.

"You're a kid. This isn't even a conversation we should be having."

"But if you're having this conversation," I say, "then you're admitting that this conversation exists and that we're having it and that means there's something to talk about."

"That doesn't even make sense," he says.

"You're my dad. It's my job to ask you to tell me the truth."

"I have."

"You haven't told me anything. You're just arguing about whether or not we should be having this conversation."

Jilly comes downstairs.

Dad says, "It's grown-up stuff."

I feel dizzy. Parents being insulting makes me dizzy. Or maybe strep throat. You choose.

"Can you take my temperature?" I ask.

Jilly races to the bathroom cabinet and grabs the ear thermometer. She loves doing this, so I just sit and wait for her to tell me.

"A hundred and one," she says, then puts the thermometer in my other ear. "And a hundred and one point five."

"I'll get you some medicine," Dad says.

"I won't be mad at all about Hawk Mountain," Jilly says.

"Thanks," I say. I lie on the couch and Jilly finds our

favorite cartoons—new episodes because Dad has cable TV. She gets me a glass of orange juice and gets my pillow from my bed. She sits on the floor by my head and asks me every commercial break if I need anything or if I'm okay.

The whole time, Dad sits in the kitchen texting on his phone.

I wish he was disco dancing again. Or singing off-tune. Or anything that made me feel like we were still as close as we were this morning.

....

By the time Sunday afternoon comes and Jilly and I are packed and ready to go back to Mom's, Dad seems like he can't wait to drop us at home. We had a good night last night. A movie and popcorn and strep-throat charades.

I watch him hurry around the house making sure we haven't forgotten anything. My fever is gone again and I feel okay. But while I watch him, I feel hot all over, like my anger is some sort of bacteria that's always there, like an infection.

Chapter 25 — Untitled Jilly

Dad drops us off outside of the house and doesn't turn the car off or anything.

He asks if we have all our stuff, he asks it a second time, and then says, "See you in two weeks!" before we close our car doors.

He turns the car around in front of the garage and drives down the lane too fast. If Lou was here he'd say, *Take it easy!* because Lou hates when anyone drives too fast down the lane. He almost got into a fistfight with the UPS delivery driver once over it. Or that's what he says. I don't think Lou would fistfight anyone.

Mom opens the door and gives us hugs. "How was that?"

"Good," I say. "Still kinda sick so I just did homework and watched cartoons."

"Oh," Mom says. "I thought you were going for a hike. Hawk Mountain and then ice cream, that's what Dad told me."

"He didn't text to tell you my fever came back?" I ask.

"No."

"Her fever was a hundred and one point five so we

stayed home and watched TV," Jilly says from behind a book. "I didn't feel like a hike anyway."

Mom puts the back of her hand on my forehead. "How do you feel?"

"Tired, but okay."

"Did you take your medicine today?"

I didn't. Crap. "Uh, no. And I don't know where it is."

Mom and I look through my backpack and Jilly's backpack and we can't find the packet of pills. I feel bad because I don't want her to have to text Dad. Not now that I know he has a big bed and new clothes and Mom doesn't know anything.

She texts him. He texts back. She texts back. He texts back.

"He's going to drop them down in ten minutes," she says. "Let's get you feeling better in the meantime." She takes my temperature. She gives me more fever medicine. She makes me a bed on the couch and I lie there feeling every shade of every color. I don't like secrets.

When I hear Dad driving down the lane again, I kneel by the window and look out. He's laughing at something. I'm kinda jealous that he's laughing now and didn't laugh much while we stayed there over the weekend.

He turns the car around and then parks. Then he hops out and walks to the back door and leaves the box on the bench that's outside. Jilly joins me at the window. We watch as he gets back in the car and takes off.

Jilly says, "Who's he talking to?"

"Probably singing to something," I say.

"Seems happy," she says.

We're lined up by the window that looks down the lane toward Lou's house. And right before Dad takes the turn to go around the corner in the lane, a head pops up in the passenger's seat.

I hope Jilly didn't see that.

"Did you see that?" she says.

"See what?"

"He had someone with him."

"Nah. It's just the trees playing a trick. Sometimes if the light goes . . ."

"I saw it with my own eyes." She looks at me sternly.

"Okay."

"You saw it too, didn't you?"

"Maybe."

Jilly goes quiet. Extra quiet. I do, too. She looks at me and frowns. It's a grown-up frown, like she's thinking really deep about things. This isn't Old Jilly. This isn't New Jilly.

We both sit on the couches in the living room and read books until dinner. And when Mom says, "What do you two want to do tonight?" Jilly and I say we want to keep reading and then go to bed.

An hour later, while Jilly takes her Sunday-night bath, Mom calls me to the kitchen window. "Lib, you have to see the moon tonight. It's huge!"

I stay under a blanket on the couch. "Seen one full moon, seen them all," I say.

Mom sighs. "You okay?"

"I don't know."

She nods. "Jilly told me Dad was grumpy today."

"Grumpy. Whatever. He's just Dad," I say. "Was he ever nice?"

"Oh, come on. You know Dad is nice," she says. "But he was always kinda . . . messy, I guess."

She doesn't know the half of how messy. Bringing a woman to our house and hiding her in the car like that.

"Is that really why you broke up?" I ask. "Just him being messy?"

"You know, one day I'll be able to tell you all that stuff but you're too young right now, Lib. I know how mature you are but it's still not right to tell you all our ugly stuff."

"True," I say.

I know there's more to it. There's got to be a big reason parents get divorced and Dad being *unwell* wasn't reason enough.

"How about we watch a movie?" she says. "I know one you'd love. About space. It's got a bit of a love scene in it but we can fast-forward."

Yes, please. Fast-forward through all love scenes forever.

Chapter 26 — Mom and Her Hatchet

Nothing happens until July.

I mean, stuff happened but nothing special. Mom still sees Rosemary every Wednesday. I still see Jan once a month. School ended and I'll go to middle school in the fall. By the time June came, most of the sixth grade class was talking to me again after Leah and Mike got recess-divorced. Finn Nolan bummed my homework off me a few more times, and he was nice about it.

I never went back to the *R* section in the library.

I never got the ring.

I never told Mom about any of it.

Now it's camp season. The idea is: Sleep outside as often as possible until it's too cold to do it anymore. Or, at least, Mom, Jilly, and I were going to aim to get as close to that as we could. Dad still hadn't taken us camping since he moved out, but he didn't cancel any more weekends, so that was cool.

The only thing about camping that makes me home-sick, and I've never been homesick while I was camping before, is the rock. Can't just lug around 130 pounds for no real reason. So I leave the meteorite at home and in a way it's a relief because it's the only thing that knows about Leah's ring.

....

"Why don't you go out on dates?" Jilly asks Mom.

Mom stands by the fire pit at the campground, hatchet in hand, and looks at the sky. "I don't know, Jill. Can't say I want to go on any dates, really."

"Why not?" Jilly asks.

"I guess I'm not ready. Or something," Mom says. "I can't even imagine what going on dates is like. Your dad and I met naturally, you know? Like the way those two trees happened to grow next to each other." She points at the woods around our campsite.

"Probably someone planted the trees, Mom. Like going on dates."

"Maybe."

"Stop asking Mom about her business," I say. "Help me put the tent up."

Mom splits two big logs into eight perfectly uniform fire starter logs. Looks up at us and says, "The world isn't all about dating and boys or whatever, you know. I have other things to do." She looks like she wants to say more, but she cleaves another part of the log in two.

"Can I try?" I ask.

She hands me the hatchet and I stand a log on its edge. With all my strength, I bring the blade down on the wood and I barely put a nick in it. I pull the hatchet out and try again. Jilly starts laughing at me and I hand the hatchet back to Mom.

She gets the hatchet two inches into the log and says, "It's not you. It's the log. There's a knot." She leaves the hatchet in the log and grabs another log. "Hold that steady for me, okay?"

I hold the handle of the hatchet while she beats the hatchet into the wood with the new log. One . . . two . . . three, and the log splits in half.

"I think we're about ready to get the fire started," she says.

She says it like she didn't just do something most people we know couldn't do. As if humans were just natural-born log splitters.

She points to the deflated tent. "We need to get that up before I start dinner. You two can do it yourselves. It's one of the new ones. Practically pops up on its own."

Jilly kicks dirt. I start feeding the poles into the sleeves of the tent and tell her to get the pegs to secure it to the ground.

"I have to pee."

"Go pee then," I say.

"I can't do it *here*."

"Yes you can. Come on. You used to do it all the time!"

Mom splits another log in two.

"I don't want to get stung on the butt."

I sigh.

Mom says, "Take your sister to the bathroom. You remember where it is?"

I nod and we walk to the bathroom.

"Stop asking her about dating," I say. "You're going to ruin her weekend."

"She shouldn't be so antisocial. It's not good for her."

"You don't know anything about anything," I say. "She'll do whatever she wants when she wants. And what do you know about dating anyway?"

....

Five minutes later we arrive back and Mom has the fire going and she's fanning it with a paper plate. The tent is exactly how we left it, which is no surprise to me, but Jilly huffs and crosses her arms.

"Come on," I say. "If we get this up fast, you can have two extra s'mores."

The two of us have the tent up in five minutes. Jilly puts our sleeping mats down and opens our sleeping bags, then tosses our backpacks in, steps in, zips it up, and reads a book until we call her for dinner.

Mom is at peace. There is nothing like watching her cook fresh food on a fire, time it perfectly, and serve up a huge meal. And while we eat she puts a little water in the dishes she cooked with and boils them clean on the fire because that's Mom. Efficient. Always thinking ahead. Ready for whatever happens next. Ready to split logs with a bowie knife or build an emergency bivouac. Ready to get divorced, too, I guess.

Chapter 21 — Cassiopeia Rising

Jilly went to sleep hours ago and Mom is snoring softly in her camping chair with a blanket over her in front of the glowing low fire.

I'm watching Cassiopeia rise in the eastern sky. It was one of my first old constellations—easy to identify on account that it's a big W. Or M. Depends which way you want to see it. But really it's supposed to be a queen sitting on her throne. Like Mom.

To me, Cassiopeia looks like a bunch of other things. Ever since I showed it to Jilly last year and she said it looked like boobs, that's the first thing I think of. But it also looks like the bottom of an upside-down heart, the number three, and a turtle.

Tonight, these three things sit heavily beside me. The number three—that's my family now. An upside-down heart—that's my family now. And a turtle—that's me. I don't know why I think this, but I do. Maybe Jan is right about me hiding in my shell waiting for everything to go back to normal. But there is no normal. Normal is Queen Cassiopeia sitting on her throne, and there's

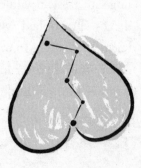

Mom, sitting in hers. Maybe this is normal. Now, I mean. Maybe this is normal now.

I miss Dad. We'd usually come back from making star maps to find Mom just like this, snoring in her chair by the fire, and I'd go to bed and the two of them would stay up and talk.

I look around the night sky and try to predict if I'll ever make a star map again. I think if something big shows itself one day, I'll start again.

I stare at the sky.

Nothing pops out.

I try harder and all I can see is me. Cassiopeia. The turtle, in her shell.

Chapter 28 — Mr. Nolan

August is the hottest month ever and the log cabin's window air conditioner isn't even helping. Jilly and I tried to get Mom to go to the community pool during the week, but instead she took us back to the campground with the good bathrooms.

"You can swim there!" she said. "They have a pond!"

....

We spent a week camping there during the hottest part of summer. By the time we got home, all Jilly and I wanted to do was wash the pond scum off ourselves and sit on the couch in front of the air conditioner unit and read or watch DVD cartoons we'd already seen.

Mom wasn't on the phone much anymore. Sometimes she asked me to take Jilly for walks to the stream and gave me a look like she had an important call to make, which I always assumed was to the lawyer who was helping her get divorced from Dad. She never talked about buying a pie and pretending she made it for anyone anymore. I think Lou lowered our rent, so maybe she gave all her pie jokes to Lou.

Jilly and I still hadn't told her about the woman in Dad's car or his new stuff.

As the month went on, including two weekends at Dad's house, it made us feel worse and worse.

....

On a random Friday afternoon, us watching cartoons in our underwear with the air-conditioning turned as cold as it could go, and Mom in her bedroom next to her air conditioner, writing an article about two new tents we tested that weekend, Mr. Nolan comes to the door. I put a pair of shorts on and Jilly covers her legs with a blanket. Since Mom is upstairs, I answer the door.

He's nicer than usual and says, "May I speak with your mother, please?" He doesn't come inside. He waits out there even though it's 103 degrees.

I get Mom, she goes out, and I hear her offer him to come in and out of the sun but he says he wants to stay out-side. I see them talking on the deck and I see Mom's face drop. Mr. Nolan puts his head in his hands and looks like he's crying. This is not the Mr. Nolan I know.

They both sit down on the deck furniture, which I know is burning their legs. Mom gets up and comes inside for a pitcher of water and two glasses. I pretend not to be watching the whole thing and I think I'm getting away with it until she says, "Liberty, stay away from the door, please?"

"Is Mr. Nolan okay?"

"He'll be fine."

"Are the boys okay? Did something happen?"

"The boys are fine. Don't worry."

This is how Mom tells us, an hour later. "I know the Nolan boys haven't been kind to you since your dad moved out. But I'm asking something of you as a favor to me, okay?"

I have no idea what she's going to say next. Jilly and I nod and agree to do whatever Mom tells us to do.

"Mrs. Nolan has moved out of the house and isn't going to come back. I want you to give those boys the kindness they didn't give you."

"Why?" Jilly asks.

I put my hand on her arm because I can see she's about to go off. New/Old Jilly goes off sometimes.

"What if they're not nice to us?" I ask.

"Then ignore them. You've been through it. You know it's hard," Mom says.

It's only August. We've only seen Dad six times since January. I didn't think we'd been through it. I was still going through it.

I stay quiet while Jilly argues. "I don't see why we have to be nice to them. We just won't be mean."

"That's a good start," Mom says.

I say, "So . . . she's never coming back? Like ever?"

"I don't know. That's what Mr. Nolan knows as of now. You know how this stuff goes. It's complicated," Mom says.

124

Jilly thinks on this for a minute. She says, "Is it okay if I'm nice to their face but really I want to punch them?"

"I think that's fine," Mom says.

....

Once we get back in front of the air conditioner and Mom goes back to work in her bedroom, Jilly says, "I feel bad for Patrick, but I don't."

"Poor Mr. Nolan. I don't even think he knows how to cook," I say.

"Or do laundry. Mrs. Nolan was always hanging out the clothes."

"Finn told me that Mr. Nolan didn't let her use the dryer if it was sunny out. Not even in winter," I say.

Jilly screws up her face. "Well, no wonder she left!"

I can't tell Jilly that it's more complicated than that. I can't tell her that everything is more complicated than what we think. Not just because we're kids, but because all this marriage and divorce stuff is weird. One minute Jilly is New Jilly—confident and going off about her opinions— the next she's in my room, sitting next to the rock, and crying because she misses our old life.

Polaris always points north. It's one of the only things I can count on. Every night it returns to the sky and does its job.

If people were more like Polaris, maybe things wouldn't be so complicated.

Chapter 29 — Jilly's Tenth Birthday

Dad has us for the weekend of Jilly's birthday but Jilly says she wants to be with Mom on the actual day, so welcome to the most awkward conversation ever.

Dad is in our kitchen—his old kitchen. Mom is also in our kitchen. She's making a pitcher of iced tea—the real kind. Jilly is sitting on the bottom step, acting like a girl whose birthday is tomorrow. I'm in the living room sitting crisscross on the floor, facing the kitchen.

Dad says, "Well, I can bring you back on Saturday I guess, and pick you up again after the party?"

"Jilly was hoping you might want to come to her birthday party. Sorry it's last minute," Mom says.

"She only told us yesterday," I say.

Dad thinks. "We can have the party at my house."

"That's a good idea," Mom says.

"I don't think it's a good idea," I say. "Not at all. Not even a little bit."

Jilly agrees. "Yeah. I want my party to be here."

"How many people?" Dad asks.

"Just us," Jilly says.

"No friends?" Dad asks.

"Liberty *is* my friend," Jilly says.

"So you want me to be here for your birthday?" Dad asks.

Mom looks nervous. Dad looks like he's running on a treadmill. Jilly still looks like a girl whose birthday is tomorrow. I don't know how I look. I'm trying to picture the four of us being here together and doing birthday things and it's too soon.

It's just too soon.

Once Mom and Dad agree to throw Jilly a party at our house, we go to Dad's. More and more decorative things have arrived around his house.

Dad is grilling dinner outside and Jilly says, "I can't wait to see what I got! I hope I get a hamster."

"You asked for a hedgehog," I say.

"Right. So I hope I get a hamster, at least. Or a gerbil. I'm not picky."

"That's good," I say.

"What'd you get me?" she asks.

"If I told you, then I'd ruin the secret." I got her a book on how to care for a hamster. Mom told me it was a good choice. Jilly is totally getting a hamster.

"Could you guys set the table?" Dad asks from the patio door.

I tell Jilly I'll do it and go to the kitchen. No lipstick on any glasses this time. But there's a new mug. It says, WELL-BEHAVED WOMEN RARELY MAKE HISTORY. I push it to the back of the mug shelf and get glasses for dinner, plates, and forks.

He has a new napkin holder that says, WIPE YOUR MOUTH!

Dad doesn't care about wiping his mouth. But someone else must. And I know it's a woman.

....

Jilly wakes me up on her birthday at six thirty in the morning. I was already awake, kinda.

"Happy birthday!" I say. Jilly jumps up and down and then runs to Dad's room and jumps on his bed.

"Wake up! Wake up! Wake up! Today is the day I get a hedgehog!"

We eat breakfast and Jilly can't stop talking. Nonstop talking. She talks so much I can't tell if she's excited or nervous. It's her birthday so I think she's excited. This is a whole new Jilly. Again. She's just evolving, like everything is normal, while I feel stuck in time, heavy as the rock.

....

We go to Mom's house—our house—whatever-I'm-supposed-to-call-it—at noon. Mom has decorated the place with balloons and a big sign that she made that says, HAPPY BIRTHDAY! There are snacks in bowls on the kitchen table. The pitcher of iced tea is out, alongside a pitcher of lemonade, Jilly's favorite.

"Welcome!" she says, as if this isn't our house.

Jilly jumps into her arms. Dad stands by the back door. Then Mom welcomes him in, too, puts her arm around him and gives him a squeeze. He smiles. She smiles. My brain forgets for a split second that none of this is real, and

I smile because it feels so good to have the four of us back in one place. Back at home.

But then I remember reality.

I blurt out that I have to poop when I don't really have to, and I jog upstairs to the bathroom. Once I hear Jilly nonstop talking, I sneak out of the bathroom and go to my room.

"This is all so weird," I say to the rock.

"It sure is."

"I feel like the gravity is messed up. I'm either floating and don't feel anything or I'm so heavy I can barely walk."

"Maybe you should see a doctor," the rock says.

"I'm not sick."

"I was kidding."

"I didn't know you could do that," I say.

"I'm you. And you're funny. Remember?"

"I guess," I say.

"Liberty! Come down!" Jilly says. "It's present time!"

"Do it for Jilly," the rock says.

I go downstairs. Dad is on the red couch with a glass of iced tea. Mom is sitting next to him with a glass of iced tea. They're holding their iced teas in opposite hands and their other hands are inches away from each other. I stare at their hands. I try, with my mind, to make them hold hands, but it's not working.

Jilly is jumping around the living room saying all kinds of stuff. "I don't want you to feel bad if you got me a gerbil because it's close enough and hedgehogs are certainly cuter, but it's okay. And Thomas in my class says that his mom and dad accidentally got him a male and a female hamster and they thought they were two females and well, you know what happened then. They had babies. And then Thomas's mom had to call the pet store and demand that they take the baby hamsters and Thomas was sad because they were so cute! Can you imagine having baby hamsters? So cute." She stops to breathe. "But I guess you can imagine because you had us and we were cute once, too."

"Hey," I say. "I'm still cute."

"You're going into middle school," Jilly says.

"So now I can't be cute anymore?"

"Not as cute as baby hamsters, no," Jilly says. And then she says, "Anyway, Thomas's mom wanted to trade in the male hamster for a female but the store wouldn't let them so then he had to get another cage, but the hamsters were sad, so he put the two of them together when his mom wasn't there and you know what happened?"

She's got this smile. Like she knows she's telling a good story. Like she knows she's got the spotlight and it's her birthday and I guess she's right. But for me, the spotlight is on Mom and Dad, sitting on the same couch sipping iced tea, almost holding hands.

"They had more babies! So Thomas's mom had to call the pet store again and that time she wanted the store to pay her for the babies because they were going to sell them anyway, to new people who wanted a hamster."

Mom and Dad are nodding. I'm still standing here

trying to figure out if because I'm going to middle school next week, I'm not cute anymore.

"Let's do presents!" Mom says. That's finally what shuts Jilly up.

Jilly sits on the floor and I make my way to the green couch and sit there trying to figure out what comes after cute.

....

Jilly gets a hamster for her birthday, in a big plastic hamster environment that has tunnels between the rooms. She's so happy.

Dad says, "We'd have gotten you a hedgehog but they're illegal in Pennsylvania."

"I know," Jilly says.

I laugh. "So you knew they were illegal?"

"Yeah. I just asked anyway. I don't know. I'm weird!"

We play games. Jilly made a pin-the-tail-on-the-hedgehog poster and we all take turns getting blindfolded and spun and trying to pin the tail. Jilly wins. I think she was peeking out of the blindfold, but it's her birthday so none of us say anything.

She keeps talking nonstop. It's like Old Jilly turned to New Jilly turned to Newer Jilly, and now it's New-Improved-Never-Stops-Talking New Jilly. She's funny again. She's stopped caring about what people think. I wish I was ten.

....

At the end of the party, games played, cake eaten, we go back to Dad's house and nothing feels right. The party turns into a bad idea. First, Jilly had to leave the hamster at

Mom's house. That's not fair. You can't give a girl a hamster and then ask her to drive away from it when the party's over. Second, Mom and Dad hugged each other goodbye. They actually hugged. Dad pecked a little kiss on Mom's cheek when it was over and Mom said something into his ear, and my brain got all confused.

In the back seat of Dad's car, on the way back to his house, all I can think about is Mom and Dad getting back together again. Even though it's not possible. Even though I know it wouldn't work out, I can't stop myself from thinking about all the ways it could work out.

I even get excited about it. I can feel inside my body how happy I would be. I almost cry happy tears when I imagine Dad moving back in. I see future camping trips. I see everything.

When we get back to Dad's, he's in a great mood. It's got to be because he loves Mom. Of course they can't really break up. They just needed a seven-month break, that's all. Some people do that.

"Clear night," Dad says.

"Yeah," I say.

"Feel like a star map?"

I shake my head. "I don't have my pencils."

"I have pencils," Dad says.

"I can't," I say. And I start to cry but I go to the bathroom as fast as I can so he doesn't see. When I come out, I say I'm going outside for a while by myself.

I lie on the grass behind Dad's town house and look up at the sky.

"If there's any way you can get my parents back together, please do," I say. I feel guilty asking. "They don't hate each other or anything. And Jilly and I really need them."

I cry some more. I don't know why. I keep seeing that hug. It was different from any other hug they had. I wonder if Mom felt it, too.

"Thanks for sending the meteorite," I say. "It's a good friend. But I'd really like if you could just do this for me. I'd make sure to never get in trouble again. I'd never be mean or curse at anyone. Ever."

The stars send a message.

All of them form the shape of a huge diamond ring.

Part Four:

BARGAINING WITH STARS

Chapter 30 — School Shopping in a Nebula

It's not elementary school anymore so nobody sends us a letter about what we might need for school. Mom and I looked at my schedule on the computer and I'll have seven classes a day. All with different teachers. I picture myself trying to hold seven books and seven notebooks and trying to get to my classes in three minutes between bells. I think about how much I'll miss recess. I think about how much I'll miss Jilly even though she can be too clingy sometimes.

"You're going to get a boyfriend," she says to me. "And then you're gonna be kissing and going on dates and holding hands and stuff."

"I'm not getting a boyfriend."

"Or a girlfriend, I guess," she says.

"I'm not getting a girlfriend, either."

"Eventually you will," she says. "And eventually you'll be holding hands and kissing."

"You sound like those girls who used to get married at recess. Don't be one of those, okay?"

"I already got married at recess," Jilly says. "Twice."

"Twice?"

"First time it didn't work out so well. Dylan What's-his-face. The one who moved to Alaska."

"Wasn't he, like, first grade?"

"Yep. First grade. We got a legal divorce before he had to move. The recess lady told us she put her stamp on it," she says. "That way we could move on and find another spouse."

"Oh, Jilly," I say. "Please stop thinking about boys and getting married. You're ten!"

She shrugs. "Seems normal to me. Everybody else is doing it."

I am definitely from another planet.

....

Mom takes us to the store for school supplies. Jilly has her list and gets all her stuff inside of five minutes and then begs to go to the toy section even though she knows she can't get any toys.

I want a cool lunch bag that's insulated and there's one with a nebula on it. Mom sees me looking at it and says, "Do you like it?"

"My old one is fine," I say.

"That's not what I asked."

"It's cool," I say. "But it's, uh." I can't figure out how to say this because it's irrational. The lunch bags are divided into two sections. This one is in the "boys" section. Nebulae are boy stuff, I guess. In middle school.

"You should get it if you like it," Mom says, and tosses it into the cart. "If you change your mind, you can always put it back."

All I can think of is Leah Jones telling me I have a boy's lunch bag. I don't know why I care so much.

The binders are simpler. Just colors. Bright and simple. I grab two and a pack of notebook paper and two spiral notebooks. Mom asks if I need index cards. "Sure," I say, all the while looking at the lunch bag.

After I get some pencils and a sharpener, Mom and I go to the toy section but Jilly isn't there.

I check all the aisles twice and Mom checks the video game aisle and I run through the other places Jilly likes to look and she's not anywhere.

I'm over by the frames and pillows when I hear Mom call, "Jilly! Jilly!"

Her voice sounds like she's never hiked a single trail in her life. Like she's never chopped wood with a bowie knife.

I find Mom and say, "You go to the checkout. Sometimes she goes up there to look at gum."

I take off toward the men's section and I call her name. I round the corner to the underwear and women's clothes. I look between the gym clothes and the socks. I pivot and go back to the toy section in case I missed her the first time. She's not there.

I take off toward the grocery section.

I can't find her anywhere. But then I hear her giggling.

The pet food.

That's where I find her.

She pulls me in close.

"Dad's here. With his girlfriend. He's hiding," she says.

I grab her by the arm and say, "Make this look real. I'm going to pretend to be mad at you, okay?"

I yank her down the main aisle of the store and Mom sees us coming because she's peeking her head up and around the racks of candy and gum and magazines.

After Mom whisper-yells at Jilly and Jilly cries real tears at the checkout, the checkout lady gives me and Jilly stickers and Mom a sympathetic look.

The whole way home, we're as quiet as roadkill.

....

Later, in my room, while Jilly pets the meteorite, I ask, "Was she pretty?"

"Not as pretty as Mom."

"Was she nice?"

"She didn't say anything," Jilly says.

"What were they shopping for?"

"I don't know. Shampoo or something?"

"What were you doing in the shampoo aisle?"

"I wanted to see if there was hair dye. I want blue hair for fifth grade."

I look at her like she's irrational.

"I never told you because I knew you'd look at me that way," she says.

"How was she less pretty than Mom?"

Jilly thinks about this a second. "I don't know. She was . . . like . . . she was all floofy. Not like Mom."

"Floofy?"

"She was wearing flats," Jilly says. "With little bows on the tops of them." She looks conflicted for a minute, like she doesn't want to judge or compare. "She was just different, is all."

"Was Dad nice, at least?"

"He was mad that I was by myself. I told him you guys were in the next aisle so I wouldn't get in trouble," she says. "Then he rushed me to the pet food aisle and ran off with her to hide."

None of this is right. Not Dad being scared to see us at the store. Not Jilly roaming around. Not both of us hiding the information from Mom that Dad has a girlfriend.

Chapter 31 — Smeelings

Lou has a fire pit down by the stream but we don't use it much because the mosquitoes are relentless down there. But sometimes Mom has to cook on a fire and tonight is one of those nights.

The stars come out while we eat. Jilly looks up more than I do. No one mentions that I should be looking up, too. Plus, I know what the stars will show me if I look up. I know I made a deal with them. I just don't know how to keep my side of the bargain. Especially now that Dad was in the store with his girlfriend.

"What are you looking forward to most?" Mom asks Jilly.

"Lunch and recess," Jilly says. This is her standard answer. Jilly loves school and hates school. It's a running battle. Mom and I stay quiet until she offers something that isn't a joke. "I like social studies, I guess."

"I wonder what you'll learn this year," Mom says.

"I hope they don't divide us into girls and boys again to talk about periods and stuff. That was boring. And embarrassing."

"You shouldn't be embarrassed about getting your period one day," I say.

"I'm not. I'm just embarrassed that they had to separate us! I mean, why can't boys learn about periods? And why can't girls learn about boy things? Wouldn't it be better to know about each other?"

Neither of us answers because Jilly has entered the New-Jilly place-of-no-pauses. She talks constantly.

"Isn't it cool that the trees might be talking to each other now? I mean, all these trees and they're probably saying that the smoke from the fire smells bad or that they miss the moon or that they miss their friends who got pulled out in the storm last summer." She breaks only to breathe. "You know, my feet keep peeling and I don't know why. They don't itch so I don't think it's athlete's foot. I hope they stop peeling soon because it's weird. Also, did you know that there's a new kind of soap that's made of ashes or something? They say it makes pimples go away. Maybe you might need that one day, Lib. Not to say you're going to be all pimply but that's what they told us in that assembly—that one day soon we'd get pimples and I thought, well Liberty doesn't have any yet so I'm probably safe for another few years. Did you get your period yet?"

"No," I say.

"Well, then I'm safe from that too. Mom, can I ask you a weird question? Does it hurt to have a tampon inside your body?"

I hold back laughter because Jilly is so free and I used to think it was because she was a kid but now I realize that it's because she's just like that. Mom doesn't laugh at all. She just says, "Nope. You don't even feel it." I'm glad Jilly asked because I was wondering, too.

Jilly takes a big breath like she's going to keep her monologue running until I'm in college, but Mom turns to me and says, "What about you? What're you most looking forward to?"

I can't be like Jilly. It's not that I don't want to tell the truth, but the truth is wrong. That's the best way I can say it. The truth is wrong. No more stars, no more dreams. All I can think about school is how I have to get the ring back to Leah Jones and how Finn Nolan will be at the bus stop with me every day from now on, just the two of us. I try to picture myself being friends with Finn again, but it's hard because even though he was nice about me loaning him my homework, I'm worried that he'll be super mean now that his family is going through what our family is going through.

"Probably biology?" I say.

Jilly gets a marshmallow from the bag and puts it on a stick and over the flames. The marshmallow goes on fire and she blows it out, stuffs it in her mouth, and chews as if she likes it. Now she's trying to be me. I'm the one who likes burnt marshmallows.

"Dad has a girlfriend," I say.

Mom stays quiet.

Jilly stops chewing and looks at me. Looks at Mom. Bursts into tears.

"I'm sorry," I say. "But I couldn't *not* tell you that."

Mom's holding Jilly now. Jilly's calmed down because

she wants to hear what Mom says. Mom doesn't look hurt. She doesn't look mad. She looks something else. I can't figure it out.

"How'd you find out?" she asks.

"I saw them at the store," Jilly says. "In the pet food aisle."

Mom nods her head. Then she shakes her head. She looks at me.

"Jilly says she's not as pretty as you," I say.

"Not even close," Jilly says. "And she doesn't look like she knows how to collect kindling or gut a fish, either."

Mom smiles. "I never much liked gutting fish."

"I don't even like eating fish," Jilly says. "I'm glad we don't have to anymore. And I never liked fishing, either. Patrick says we shouldn't be living without a dad but I'd do okay if I never had to eat fish again."

Mom takes a long breath. "Does Patrick think that women just shrivel up and die when they don't have men? Probably. Is he wrong? Definitely."

Jilly and I stay quiet.

"And I won't make you eat fish ever again," Mom says.

"How long have you known?" I ask.

"I haven't liked fishing ever, really. But your dad did, and I'm not one to step in the way of another person's happiness."

"But you knew, right? About the girlfriend?" I ask. I still don't know why adults change the subject so much.

She gives me the look she gives when something isn't right to talk about in front of Jilly. Something in it tells me that Dad's girlfriend isn't new. Something in it makes me an adult who changes the subject.

"Stop just eating marshmallows," I say to Jilly. "Let's make Mom the best s'more ever."

"I have the perfect thing!" Jilly says. She races into the house and leaves Mom and me by the fire.

"Sorry," I say.

"Nothing to be sorry for. I wish he'd have found a better way to tell you is all."

"I'm still sorry," I say.

"I want you to have a good year in school and get used to this new arrangement. It's been almost eight months since he moved out. We had a good summer, yeah?"

I feel instant shame. I didn't have a good summer. I just had a summer.

"What?" she asks.

Jilly is still talking as she runs from the back door of the house, over the deck, down the steps, and toward the fire pit. She has a Reese's Peanut Butter Cup in her hand and she's waving it in front of her face. She stops and stands still and smells the air and says, "You know, campfires give me serious smeelings. I'm gonna miss summer."

"Smeelings?" Mom asks.

"Smells that make feelings," Jilly explains.

"I kinda want to wear this sweatshirt on the first day of school just to smell like camping," I say.

Three days to school. I feel lighter now that we all know that Dad has a girlfriend. I hope the stars will keep their side of the deal. Life will go back to normal. I can go back to being Old Liberty.

....

I sit with the meteor before bed.

"I'm going to return the ring," I say.

The meteorite says, "Good plan."

"I think Mom and Dad will get back together. They're meant to be together," I say.

"Ya think?"

"Yep."

The rock says, "But what about the girlfriend?"

"I don't know. She probably isn't really his girlfriend."

"Be careful," the rock says.

"What? Is she an ax murderer or something?" I ask.

"Just be careful about what you're thinking, okay?" the rock says.

"You're from space. Stars are in space. You always tell me the truth and the stars have never lied, either. I know what I'm doing, okay?"

The rock says, "Okay."

Chapter 32 — The Scarecrow with Boobs

Dad called us after dinner on Tuesday, the night before the first day of school. He talked to Jilly for about three minutes—well, she talked to him—and then she passed the phone to me.

"You ready for tomorrow? My little girl in middle school. Hard to believe."

"Yep."

"You know what saved me when I went to middle school? I paired up with the biggest kid I knew—"

"Bobby Heffner. You've told me that story before. I don't think I'll need a bodyguard, but thanks anyway."

"You scared?"

"Nope."

"You okay?"

"Sure. I'll see you soon," I said, ready to hang up.

"Whoa. Hold on. Where's my Liberty?"

I didn't like any part of that question. I'm not his Liberty. I'm my Liberty. I mean, look at my name—it actually means that.

"See you soon, Dad."

"I love you," he said. "Have a great first day, okay?"

I hung up.

....

The first day of middle school was like landing on a new planet. There were bells and late passes and bathroom passes and a locker that always seemed too far away from the room where I had to be next.

But I did it. I got on the bus home. When I got in, Mom asked me how it was.

"I don't know. It was weird," I said.

"Did you see any old friends?"

"Not really. There's a bunch of new kids from the other elementary schools. I'm sure I'll make new friends."

"Teachers seem nice?"

"So far," I said.

"You coming for the walk to pick Jill up?" she asked.

"I just want to take a nap."

"You look so tired. Do it."

....

I don't even remember what we had for dinner last night.

Middle school is probably going to kill me.

That's what I'm thinking today as I walk to the end of the lane to meet the bus at five past seven.

Finn Nolan arrives a minute after me.

I say, "Hi, Finn."

He pretends not to hear me and then we wait.

Neither of us is saying anything even though we've

known each other since diapers and I've seen him have a nosebleed and the chicken pox and he's seen me break my finger and walk into a tree and knock myself out once. Even though we're both going through something kinda similar. But neither of us says anything.

When I step onto the bus at ten past seven, Finn walks by me to go sit near the back where the high school kids are. He looks like a different Finn Nolan. As we drive to school, I wonder if I've looked like a different Liberty Johansen for the last eight months, too.

....

I'm only late to Spanish class today. And I have a pass, so I'm not even technically late. I almost have my locker stops figured out and I feel more confident about where the bathrooms are.

During lunch, I go to the bathroom closest to the cafeteria, and standing at the mirror, drawing eyeliner around her eyes, is Leah Jones. Pretend-president of our old sixth grade class.

Finn Nolan and Leah Jones on the same day. The building suddenly feels the size of a garden shed.

I say, "Hi."

She doesn't say anything.

I go into a stall and listen for her to leave but she doesn't. I get a little scared, but I stop myself. I think of the sound of running water and I finally pee. I get out, wash my hands in the sink farthest from Leah, and then I go back to lunch.

....

Mid–algebra class the classroom phone rings and Mr. Algebra tells me to head down to the main office. When I get there, I see Finn Nolan sitting in a chair. I sit down next to him.

"Hey," I say.

"Hey."

"Do you know what this is about?"

"What what's about?" he asks.

"Why we got called down?"

Finn looks at me like he doesn't know what I'm talking about, but before I can say more, I'm called into the vice principal's office.

This guy is *not* Ms. S. from planet elementary school. This guy is far scarier. Bald. Mean-looking. Serious.

"Liberty," he says. "I'm Mr. Scott."

"Hi?" I manage.

"Do you know why you're here?"

"No idea," I say.

"You sure?"

"I had a pass when I was late to Spanish today," I say.

"Where were you during lunch?"

"Eating lunch. I sit with some kids I don't really know yet," I say.

"Did you take a trip to the ladies' room?"

"Yeah. When I finished lunch," I say.

He looks at me in a way that Ms. S. used to look at me. I think school principals and vice principals must read a lot of detective books. "And then what?"

"Then I washed my hands and went back to the cafeteria," I say.

"Did you see anyone on the way?"

"Not anyone I knew," I say, thinking of who I saw in the halls on the way to and from the bathroom. But then of course I realize he's talking about Leah. "Oh. Leah Jones was in the bathroom the whole time I was there. She was putting makeup on."

When bald people raise their eyebrows, they kind of look like puppets.

"What?" I ask.

"I know you've had a habit of drawing on school walls before now, so I'm wondering if you drew on any today."

"All I have is pencils and this one pen," I say.

More puppet faces, then he says, "Let's take a walk."

We walk to the guidance office first where I stand staring at the anti-bullying box they told us about in homeroom the first day. Then Mr. Scott introduces me to a woman—a guidance counselor. He tells me her name and I forget it the minute he says it. We get to the ladies' room outside the cafeteria and she and I walk in together and she shows me the inside of the stall where I'd peed at lunch.

A bunch of dots. A bunch of dots connected in crude Sharpie marker, pretending to be a star map.

"Ugh!" I say. "Whoever drew that has never even looked up!"

The woman looks surprised. "What do you mean?"

"It's just dots, you know?"

She crosses her arms and nods as if she knows what I'm talking about, but I can tell from her face she has no idea.

"What's it even supposed to be?" I say. "Looks like a scarecrow with boobs."

....

Mr. Scott believes me—probably because I can't stop talking about how star maps are supposed to be based on accurate star placement. You can't just put some dots on paper and connect them. That's what I tell him.

"You have a real interest in this stuff," he says. We say goodbye to the lady with no name at the guidance office and walk back to his office and close the door.

"I've been drawing stars since I was little," I say.

He hands me a piece of paper and a pen. "Draw some for me."

I start with Polaris. "North Star," I say. I ink the rest of the stars in Ursa Minor and then move down to Ursa Major because once people see the Big Dipper, they usually show some sort of interest.

"Hey! That's the Big Dipper!" he says. Right on time.

"Do you want me to draw in Boötes? Or can we stop now?"

His puppet features look amused. I like him.

"I used to teach science," he says. "Mostly chemistry. But back in college I was part of the astronomy club."

"Sounds cool."

He points to the paper. "That's a pretty hard thing to do."

"I have hundreds of them." I pause. I'm about to tell

Mr. Scott about my dream—to change the way people look at the stars—but then I remember I gave up on that. "Can I go back to class now?"

He nods, and when I get up and turn to go he says, "You know, our science wing walls could use something interesting. The art wing has all the fun."

I just walk out because I don't know what to say and because the thought of drawing star maps on the science wing makes me think of how much I miss elementary school. And Dad.

....

Middle school handles people like Leah Jones different from Ms. S. over at West El. No more apologies or meetings where two kids have to talk things out. When I'm in line for the bus, I hear Leah got detention.

On the bus, Finn Nolan still looks like a different Finn Nolan. His hair hasn't been cut since summer and his bangs hang in his eyes. It's like he's trying to hide.

When I get home, I'm tired again. Like I just hiked the Appalachian Trail. Mom tells me to take another nap. She says, "Don't look so worried. It's just a new schedule. Your body will get used to it."

When I close my eyes the only stars I see are Leah Jones's random dots—like the scarecrow with boobs is going to haunt me forever. I barter with the stars inside my eyelids. I tell them that I'll have the ring back by the end of the week.

Chapter 33 — Standardized Tests Are Stupid

I'm so used to middle school already that it's weird. Classes aren't hard and the people are pretty nice. I like the new kids from the other elementary schools. At lunch, I miss Malik and I hope people are being nice to him back at West El, and I sit with a girl named Maya who's from North El. She lives on a farm. We have a lot in common. Mostly, we don't talk about boys, clothes, or makeup.

Mom and I pick Jilly up together on the fifth day of school.

Jilly gets off the bus crying.

"It was red. All red!" she says.

Mom and I look confused and she explains. "The tests. On the computer. Math. I got all red."

I've been here. Last year I had a lot of red in my reading section because even though I read a lot, I didn't answer the questions the way they wanted me to. "They give you hard questions so you get red," I say. "It's not you, it's the questions."

Mom looks angry. "They give you guys a standardized test during the first week of school?"

"I'm dumb!" Jilly says.

"You're not even close to dumb," Mom says. "I have two smart, imaginative kids and all the school wants to do is make them like everybody else. I will never understand what the hell is going on with education."

Mom knows she just said the H-word. She doesn't care. The H gives me and Jilly a home. Like warm, cozy bunk beds, H. I get the top bunk. Jilly gets the bottom bunk, and Mom is the H, made of some kind of strong wood that even she can't split with a hatchet.

....

Three more days until we have our next Dad weekend. Jilly thinks he's going to let us meet his new girlfriend. Every time she says *new* in front of *girlfriend* I want to tell her the truth but she's ten and I'm not and she's already sad because of her test results. She says the meteorite makes her feel better, so we're in my room.

"I wonder if she's going to be one of those stepmoms who buys us cool stuff."

"Why do you want a stepmom anyway?" I ask.

"I don't," Jilly says. "I don't even want a stepmom. I just—I'm trying to—I don't know. Think positive or something?"

"That's probably good," I say.

Jilly looks at me like she knows. I try to look other places.

"You know something I don't know," she says.

"What? No," I say, staring at a sock on the floor.

"You said it this summer. When we were there. You knew then, didn't you?"

"Not really. I just suspected."

I don't tell her how the sky told me. I don't tell her about the wineglass. Plus, by next week, we'll have Dad back if I keep up my side of the deal.

"How's the library back at West El?" I ask.

"That's a weird question," Jilly says.

"I miss Mrs. Hanson. We don't have special classes anymore. The library is there, but some people never go to it."

Jilly screws up her face and says, "So?"

"So, what day is your library day?"

"I think we go on Monday." She looks around my room and I don't say anything because I'm formulating the next step of my plan. "Why are you so interested in the library?"

"Just tell me before your next class there, okay?"

I feel bad. But it's for the best.

Chapter 34 — Meteorites Don't Eat Hamburgers

Dad picks us up right on time on Friday. Mom gives us a hug and kiss in the kitchen and sends us to the driveway where he's waiting.

"We have reservations for six!" he says.

"Reservations for what?" Jilly asks.

"A special treat."

"Roller-skating?" she says.

"You don't need reservations for roller-skating," I say.

"I'm taking you out to eat," he says. "We're meeting a — a friend there."

"You don't have to call her a friend," I say.

"Yeah," Jilly says. "You can just say we're meeting your girlfriend."

When we get to the restaurant parking lot, Dad takes our hands as if we're in a parade. A Proud Dad parade. I want to ask him who he is.

Not to say Dad was never proud of us. I'm sure he was and he still is. But the parade of Proud Dad makes me feel like the meteorite. I don't belong here. I'm not from here. These are not my natural surroundings. Also: Dad should be with Mom.

His girlfriend is already here. Already sitting. Already sipping a glass of wine. She stands when we get near the table and smiles nervous like we might be wild animals. Or maybe that's me. Smiling nervous or wild animal, you choose.

"It's so nice to meet you both," she says. "I'm Tiffany."

Tiffany. Not a camping name.

Jilly waves and sits down. I don't know what I do because I'm so busy trying to feel like I'm from the same planet as Tiffany.

Dad sits next to her and puts his hand on her shoulder. They kiss—just a peck—and I want to throw up. Inside my meteorite brain, I say, "Why did you do that? Don't be kissing some stranger in front of us!" Inside my meteorite brain I compare that kiss with the kisses he used to give Mom. Mom's were better.

"You okay, Liberty?" Dad asks.

"Yeah. Just tired."

"Your dad tells me you just started middle school," Tiffany-alien-smelly-not-my-stepmom says.

"It's the natural progress of things," I say. Even Jilly looks at me like I'm weird. "I couldn't stay at West El forever, I guess."

"True," Tiffany says.

Dad says, "Are the classes okay? A lot of homework or what?"

"It's all fine," I say, and look down at my menu.

"Fifth grade is awesome!" Jilly says. "We had to take those stupid tests all week but now we're actually learning stuff. Like, did you know that you can't really grow an apple tree from the seeds in apples?"

Tiffany says, "I didn't know that."

"And I knew all my states. Forgot some of the capitals, but no one else knew all their states. I even remembered the difference between Colorado and Wyoming. And I could name all seven continents."

Dad is looking at me and not listening to Jilly, who's now talking about math and how fractions still confuse her. She's making up for me. I don't feel bad about it because I spent a lot of this year making up for her.

Jilly is a giant broom and I am a giant pile of broken glass.

The menu is expensive. The food is pretty fancy. There are no grilled cheese sandwiches. I find the cheapest hamburger and close my menu and look around.

Dad and Tiffany sip wine and make eyes at each other. If I was to guess, they're in love.

....

"Is the burger good?" Tiffany asks me while my mouth is full.

I finish chewing and say, "It's okay. I like them better when they're cooked on a fire. My mom makes the best ones."

Jilly wrestles with a chicken tender. Dad cringes when Jilly starts to talk with her mouth full. She says, cheek full of chicken, "Do you go camping, Tiffany?"

"Kind of. I used to, I guess. I'm not really the outdoorsy type now that I got older."

"How old are you?" Jilly asks.

Dad says, "You don't ask ladies their age."

I say, "Are you from the old days or something?" I say it for real. Not in my space-rock brain. He laughs like this is a joke, so I say, "Geez, Dad. You always told us that girls shouldn't be taught all that crap. Who cares how old Tiffany is? Jilly was just trying to make conversation."

Jilly is eating the last of her chicken tender. She says, "Yeah."

"I'm thirty-one," Tiffany says. "And they're right, Jack. Nothing wrong with women getting older."

Dad looks mad now. Tiffany notices and puts her hand on his hand and pats it.

"Dad! She's thirteen years younger than you!" Jilly says.

Tiffany laughs. Dad looks uncomfortable. Jilly keeps doing math.

"That's like if I had a boyfriend who was twenty-three!"

I think this is probably the most fun Jilly's had doing math in years.

I leave half of my burger on my plate and pick at the sweet potato fries. Tiffany asks if she can try one and I push the plate toward her a little. "Ooo! They're good!"

I want to tell her that girls in our family don't make small talk over sweet potato fries, but I just breathe. I think about the stars. I wonder if I'm thinking about stars because I'm with Dad. I want to stop thinking about stars. Tiffany would probably think I'm weird, anyway, for seeing things in the stars. She probably only wants to see what everybody taught her to see.

....

When we leave, Dad, Jilly, and I get into Dad's car and say goodbye to Tiffany, who drives some kind of Jeep. When we get back to Dad's house, things look really different. There are pictures on the walls and a tablecloth on the kitchen table. New appliances. A new sofa. When I go to Jilly's and my room and turn on the light, I'm surprised to see a bunch of my star maps on the walls, framed like they're art.

Dad's behind me at the doorway. I didn't even hear him come up the steps.

"Tiffany framed them for you. She thinks you're a genius."

"Huh," is all I can say.

Dad gave me stars. Dad took away my stars. Now here I am looking at them framed like they're modern art.

"Did Tiffany move in here or something? Everything is different," Jilly says from downstairs.

Dad looks at me. He doesn't answer Jilly.

But then Tiffany walks in the front door and answers the question for all of us.

Chapter 35 — Angry Constellation

Tiffany listens to the radio while she makes French toast for breakfast—like she lives here. I have so many angry thoughts I don't think I'll last until lunch.

The French toast is good and Dad says, "We're going to Hawk Mountain today for a hike. Then maybe a movie tonight. Sound good?"

Jilly nods and gives a thumbs-up. I shrug.

"Looks like your sister has a dose of the tweens," Dad says to Jilly.

"She hates that word, Dad."

It's such a stupid word. "So was it a dose of the tweens that made you leave us? Or how about all those weekends you didn't pick us up? Tweens, right?"

"You can't talk to me that way," he says.

"You can't talk to *me* that way," I say.

"I was just being funny."

"No. You were making fun of me because I'm a twelve-year-old girl and you think I'm too emotional or something. Get over it. Of anyone in our family, we all know that I'm not the one with the emotional problems, okay?"

Dad takes a breath like he's about to say something but then he just exhales and doesn't say anything.

By the time we're about to leave for Hawk Mountain and I'm watching Tiffany slowly lace up a brand-new pair of Outdoor World hiking shoes so she doesn't chip her manicured fingernails, I know I'm not going to make it through the day. I need to call Mom and ask her to pick me up.

I go into the kitchen, where Dad is packing snacks and lunch into his old blue backpack. I stop for a minute and think of how many times I've opened the clips on that backpack to get something he asked me to get. His knife, a flashlight, a Band-Aid, a towel to wipe his sweat while he chopped wood on camp in mid-August—all things that don't seem to fit with his new tablecloth or new cologne.

"Sorry about what I said at breakfast," he says. "I didn't mean to be disrespectful."

I keep staring at the blue backpack.

"I know I shouldn't try to be funny about stuff like that," he adds.

"Stuff like what?" I say.

"You're growing up. You're in middle school. I feel like we used to be best friends and now I don't even know you." He stops what he's doing and if I was to guess, he's about to cry. "I miss you. I'm trying to get on with my life and be happy but when I see you growing up, I feel like I really screwed up. Screwed up everything," he says.

I want to give him a hug but I don't. The hug is a tablecloth. It's hiding the scratched, messy tabletop.

"You did screw up everything," I say. "You really did."

He starts to cry. I still don't hug him.

"Can I call Mom?"

He hands me his phone and I go out the back-patio door so I can talk to her without anyone hearing.

The phone rings. And rings. And then it goes to voice-mail and at the sound of the beep I can't leave a message because I don't want her to worry.

We go to Hawk Mountain.

....

Tiffany has never been to Hawk Mountain before. I tell her that we'll probably see bald eagles and she doesn't believe me.

"She's serious, Tiff. You're gonna see a bald eagle today," Dad says.

"And a merlin or kestrel if you're lucky," Jilly says. "Bald eagles are overrated. Everybody wants to see one. But a kestrel. Now that's something."

"What about hawks?" Tiffany asks.

"You'll see a lot of those," I say. "But Jilly and I go for the weird birds. Probably because we're weird birds."

Jilly says, "Caawcaaw!"

I say, "Eeeeeeeeee!"

After all this, I'm pretty sure Tiffany still thinks we're lying about the bald eagles. Lucky for her, one of them greets us as we drive up the mountain to the parking lot.

Dad points out the windshield toward the top of the electrical pole. "Look! There's one!"

"How do you even know from here, Jack? Stop kidding around."

Jilly's leaned forward already and says, "That's a bald eagle, all right."

Tiffany stares at it. "Really?"

"Really," Dad says.

"God, it's beautiful."

Dad goes to say something probably sappy and gross about how Tiffany is beautiful too but he stops himself and concentrates on finding a parking space. We all get out and stop at the bathroom.

Tiffany can't stop looking up.

"You should pee now. It's a long trail," I say.

"I didn't even know we had bald eagles," she says.

"Come on," I say, and I take her to the last bathroom we'll see for three hours.

We take it slow to the South Lookout. It would usually only take us fifteen minutes, but we talk. Mostly Jilly, really. I learn that Tiffany is: a big fan of mystery novels and coffee ice cream. She works at some place that sells insurance or something. She left home when she was fifteen and doesn't really talk to her family.

"Not even your mom?" Jilly asks.

"Nope. Not even my mom," Tiffany answers.

"What'd you do when you ran away?" I asked.

"I didn't really run away," she says. "I just moved out and started living with my aunt and uncle. Got a job. Moved in with my boyfriend eventually."

"When you were fifteen?" Jilly asks.

"No. No—more like seventeen I think. I can't really remember. It was a hard time."

"Did you go to college?" I ask.

"No."

"Oh," I say.

"I want to try it now, but I still really don't know what I want to do," she says. "I think I want to help kids like me."

"Insurance kids?" Jilly asks.

"Kids who were homeless. Stuff like that. Bad homes."

"You were homeless?" I ask.

"There are a lot of different ways to be homeless," Tiffany says. "It's not just what they show you on TV."

"We don't watch TV," Jilly says.

"Well, then it's not just people sleeping on the street with all their stuff in bags," Tiffany says. "There are a lot of people who don't have homes. A lot of kids. Even your age," she says. "I think it's disgusting how we don't help them."

"You mean there's ten-year-olds that are homeless?" Jilly asks.

"Yep."

"That's sad."

"Yep."

"I think you should go to college and help them," Jilly says.

I don't say anything because I'm so busy wondering why I thought I knew Tiffany when I didn't know her at all. If you'd have asked me last night at dinner to write her childhood story, I'd have put her in dancing lessons and in front of department store mirrors, trying on different makeup. I'd have told you she was a cheerleader. I suddenly realize how judgmental I am.

I'm no different from Leah Jones or all the other kids who used to make fun of Malik for not being able to eat nuts. And what's so wrong with cheerleaders anyway?

We get to the South Lookout and I climb out to the rocks. Dad looks concerned because I'm quiet and jumping from boulder to boulder. I'm not doing this because of Tiffany, like Dad probably thinks. It's not about her. It's not about Dad, who's holding Jilly's hand and pointing out birds circling the valley. It's about me. And middle school. And divorce.

That's my present constellation. Me, middle school, and divorce. It's an angry constellation. It's not even glowing red. It's on fire.

I feel like I just lost a chunk of my life.

I gave up on myself.

I gave up on being an exception.

....

There are at least fifteen hawks flying around today. The eagle must have found something tasty to eat because it's gone. Jilly says, "Look!" and points.

The kestrel. So little, and yet so powerful. So common, but normal people hardly ever talk about it.

Jilly and I sit on the edge of a rock while Dad shows Tiffany the view. Now that Tiffany lives with Dad, I'm wondering if I'm too late to make things right.

"So, Monday," I say to Jilly. "I need you to do me a favor when you go to the library at school."

"Okay," she says.

"It's a secret mission."

"I'm good at those."

"You can't tell anyone about the mission," I say. "And when it's over we will never speak of it again."

"Promise."

"Okay," I say.

"What's the mission?" she asks.

"I'll tell you tomorrow night. Once we're home."

"So why are you asking me now?"

"Just wanted to make sure you're on the team," I say.

"You okay?" she asks. "Isn't it weird that Tiffany lives there now?"

"It's totally weird," I say.

Chapter 36 — Suddenly Grilled Cheese Sandwiches Are Fine

We decide to skip going to the movies. We're all tired after a whole day on the mountain. By the time we left, we were starving. I had two grilled cheese sandwiches at the diner on the way home. Tiffany had a grilled cheese sandwich, too. Dad didn't roll his eyes at either of us.

Jilly has to go to the bathroom before dessert so I go with her and she says, "She's not as bad as I thought."

I say, "Yeah. She's okay."

Jilly seems to relax when I say this because I think she looks up to me. This whole divorce business makes her watch me for cues. So I figure I better keep my cues right.

"Dad seems happy," I say.

"Yeah," she says. "I hope Mom gets a boyfriend."

"Mom doesn't need a boyfriend."

"I know. But I hope she does. You know — because it's nice to have someone to hold hands with or something."

Jilly has been married at recess twice. She probably knows what she's talking about.

When we come back from the bathroom, Dad has a bright idea about going stargazing in our old favorite spot — down by the nature reserve, where it's darker than dark if the moon isn't out, which it is. "You can show Tiff the stars. What do you think?" he says.

I know Jilly is watching me for cues.

I say yes.

....

It's a full moon, but clear. Dad puts two blankets out and Tiffany sits on one while Jilly and I lie back on ours and look up at the sky. Dad has to go back to the car for a sweatshirt and Tiffany takes the opportunity to have us alone.

"I really appreciate you girls being so nice to me this weekend," she says.

"You're nice," Jilly says. "We're nice."

I point up. "You missed it. Meteor. Two o'clock."

"Crap," Jilly says.

"You saw a *meteor*?" Tiffany says.

"Shooting star," I say. "Same thing."

"Oh. Phew. I thought you meant something else."

"I think Liberty should have a boyfriend," Jilly says.

"Shut up," I say. "Tiffany, look up. You're going to miss the next one."

Dad brings her a sweatshirt and Tiffany moves back to where Dad is and curls up in the crook of his arm. Jilly doesn't see it and I'm glad. About five minutes pass.

"Seven o'clock! Did anyone see that?" I point.

"Darn it. I was looking over there," Tiffany says.

"Missed it," Dad says.

"You need paper for a map?" he asks me.

"Nah. I don't do that anymore."

He sits up. Mission accomplished.

"I'm getting cold," Tiffany says.

"Me too," Dad says.

"I'm not," I say.

We leave anyway. As I get in the car, Dad lifts my chin so he can meet me eye to eye and I do it, but I think I look mad. I probably am mad. I don't know. I'm not dumb, but I don't need all that lovey crap right there in front of my face. Dad was never subtle about stuff, I guess.

The stars aren't subtle either. I know because I couldn't see anything in the sky tonight but the ring. I can still see Mom and Dad hugging in my head. How she whispered something in his ear. I know this whole bargain is like buying a lottery ticket, but I'm trying to think positive. Deep down, I already feel bad for Tiffany when Dad tells her he's coming back to us.

....

I fall asleep the minute I hit our bunk beds and Jilly wakes me up early because she's awake and Dad and Tiffany aren't yet.

Jilly says, "You should show her the meteorite."

"What?"

"She doesn't know anything about science."

I rub my face. "What time is it?"

"Seven."

"It's Sunday."

"So?"

"You know the rules," I say. I turn toward the wall and curl up.

"Those rules are for when we're at our house. This is different."

I try to close my eyes and fall asleep but I know Jilly's lonely. I can't leave her like that, even if I'm lonely, too.

I sit up. Hit my head on the ceiling. Say "Ouch!" as loud as I can so Dad and Tiffany will wake up. It's two weekends a month. Dad can get his Sunday sleep-ins during the two weekends he doesn't have us.

We go downstairs and Jilly puts the TV on. I put some bread in the toaster and press the lever down. Twice. Three times. Until the smoke alarm goes off and wakes everybody up.

....

By the time we drive home, Dad is chatty and normal.

"Are you gonna fight to have us part-time?" Jilly asks.

Dad is quiet.

"I think it's good the way it is," I say.

I miss Mom. Two days and I miss her. I don't know what I'd do if I'd have to spend a whole week away from her. Not like I'm not independent, but I just need her around, is all.

We take the right turn onto Lou's lane and I try to think of something else to say but I can't think of anything. I want to go to my room and tell the rock about Tiffany. I want to eat dinner with Mom. I want to sleep in my bed.

Our goodbyes are fast. Jilly gives Dad a hug and I do, too. Then Dad puts his hand out for a fist bump and I give him one but it's weird.

"You'll get used to middle school, I promise," he says.

I didn't say a thing about middle school the whole weekend. "Middle school is fine," I say.

He nods—real cool-like—and says, "Tiffany told me it can be a real hard place. That's all. And I miss my Liberty."

You'd really think he'd know what my name means by now.

Chapter 37 — My Liberty

I wonder if Dad's watch stopped on January 18 when he moved out. I think he wants me to be twelve-year-old Liberty forever.

It's complicated but it will all be over in a few weeks. I'll be able to look at the stars and maybe even make maps again. And Dad will move back in with us. Maybe Tiffany can live in Dad's town house by herself. That would probably be great for her.

....

Mom is talking to Jilly when I walk inside from Dad's car. Jilly's talking really fast and isn't really looking at Mom's face. I'm looking at Mom's face and something is wrong.

"She really didn't think we had bald eagles here!" Jilly says. "So then we saw one on the way to the parking lot. Anyway, she's nice and she makes good French toast."

"Not as good as yours, though," I say.

"Hey, kiddo!" Mom says. I give her a big hug. "You guys had a good weekend?"

"It was nice, yeah. Hawk Mountain is always good," I say. "Jilly got to see her kestrels and we went down the River of Rocks."

Mom smiles. "You can talk about Tiffany if you want."

"She's nice," I say.

"She was homeless!" Jilly says.

Mom looks surprised.

"When she was a kid," I say.

"That's horrible," Mom says.

Jilly says, "Did you know there are kids my age who're homeless?"

"It's sad," Mom says.

"I'm going upstairs," I say.

Mom's gone back to looking like something's wrong.

....

Mom tells Jilly to get her laundry together and add it to mine so she can do the wash. I flop down next to the meteorite.

"Mom isn't herself," I say.

"She's fine," the rock says.

"I think Jilly talked too much about Tiffany," I say.

"She's fine," the rock says.

"Did she cry at all this weekend?" I ask. "I'm worried that she doesn't cry."

"She cried a lot before your dad left," the rock says. "You just didn't know it."

"Huh."

Maybe I think Mom is *my* mom the way Dad thinks I'm *his* Liberty. I shouldn't expect her to do certain stuff. I should just let her be whatever she is.

....

Jilly bursts into tears before we're halfway through dinner. Old-New Jilly. She's inconsolable because she thinks that she hurt Mom's feelings by talking about Tiffany.

"I'm fine," Mom says. "Really. You don't have to feel bad at all."

"If he doesn't love you anymore, then he doesn't love us, either," Jilly cries.

Mom stops eating and thinks about that. If I was to guess, it hurt. "Love isn't something you can just turn off," she says. "Your dad and I had a lot of great years together. We have you two together and we always will. One day maybe I'll get a boyfriend, too. I won't be doing it to hurt anyone. It'll just be because I found someone nice to hang out with. That's all."

Jilly looks angry. She says, "Well it's not fair that he found someone first."

"It's not a race," Mom says.

"I just don't like that she lives there," Jilly says. "It means we'll never get Dad to ourselves again."

"We will. Or maybe we won't. Maybe we can teach Tiffany how to make a campfire and stuff like that. Or maybe she can teach us whatever she knows," I say.

Mom gets up from the table and puts the rest of her dinner in the trash can. She doesn't do it fast or angry, but something isn't right.

While Jilly and I finish dinner, she cleans out the toaster.

I say, "Jilly, can you take your bath first tonight? I need to talk to Mom about algebra."

"Sure," she says. "But remember—you promised me a bedtime story . . . about the library." She winks at me.

When I hear the bath running and Jilly's singing echoing around the bathroom I go to Mom, who's still wiping the countertops down in the kitchen. She turns to me and says, "He didn't tell me she moved in. I had no idea." And then she cries. Big tears. She sits at the kitchen table and puts her hands over her face and I stand next to her and rub her back and tell her it's going to be okay. She says she's sorry and I tell her there's nothing to be sorry about. She says, "He didn't tell me," and I say I know and that it's okay. I get her the box of tissues. Jilly keeps singing a song in her bath and doesn't know this is happening.

Mom says, "You shouldn't have to see me like this."

I say, "There's nothing wrong with crying. It's okay, Mom. It really is."

At this, she sobs out another hundred sobs and her tears drop onto the tabletop and start to make a puddle.

Time moves in a different way when you have a sobbing mother. It feels like Jilly just got into the bath but she's already in her room, still singing. I keep rubbing Mom's back and being fine.

"I don't want Jilly to see me like this," she says. "I'm going to take a walk. You go have your shower. Tell Jilly I'll tuck her in when I'm back."

"I promised her a bedtime story," I say. "Take your time. It's gonna be okay, Mom. I promise."

Chapter 38 — Bedtime Story on Planet Perfection

Jilly is excited about the mission, but she doesn't know what the mission is yet.

I say, "This is a sister mission. Totally secret, okay?"

"Of course," she says. "We covered that."

"This isn't going to make me look like a good person. But you have to let me explain."

"Just tell me the mission. I can do it," she says. "You look like you're about to cry. I don't want you to cry."

"I need you to get something from the West El library for me." I get a piece of paper and draw a diagram. "So if you go to the *R* section in fiction, you'll see this shelf," I say.

"Okay," she says.

"Right under the second shelf, this one here," I point, "you'll see three plastic circles in the wooden shelf. They're about the size of a quarter. A little bigger. They cover big holes—like a plug in a drain. Like those," I show her a smaller version in her bedside table.

Jilly nods.

I point to the one on the right. "You have to pry off this one—it'll come off easy enough if you use your student ID card or something thin and flat like that. Once you pop it off, inside will be an item," I say. I can't even say the right word. "Get the item and put the plastic circle back into its hole."

"Item?"

"It's a ring," I say.

"Whose ring is it?" she asks.

"You can't tell anyone about this," I say. "And you can't get caught."

"I won't. I already told you. Secret sister mission. I get it. But you gotta tell me whose ring it is."

I say, "Put the ring in your pocket or wherever is safe so it won't fall out. Bring it home to me and don't show it to ANYONE."

"What kind of ring is it?"

"It's like a diamond ring. Looks like a diamond ring anyway."

"Why did you hide a diamond ring?" Jilly asks.

"Long story. And from now on, let's call it the item. It's like a code word."

I look at Jilly. She looks like she knows I'm lying. But then she says, "Okay. No problem. I'll report back tomorrow with the item."

"Don't get caught," I say.

"I won't get caught."

"Don't tell anyone," I say. My stomach turns and I feel clammy.

"You sound like you robbed a bank or something."

"If you feel in any way like you're going to get caught, drop the mission."

"Yeah. Like a bank robber. That's what I was saying," she says.

"It'll all be over by tomorrow," I say. "For now, do you want some hot chocolate?"

"It's hot outside."

"Lemonade?" I wipe my palms on my shorts.

"I don't need anything," Jilly says. "It's almost bedtime. Probably not a good idea for me to drink something. I'll have to pee."

"I have to take a shower," I say. "I'll be back to read to you when I'm out."

"Where's Mom?" she asks.

"She went for a walk."

"She's mad about Tiffany."

"It's okay," I say. "It will all work out. Promise."

Jilly looks at me like I'm weird. I guess I am weird. I made a deal with the stars and that's probably weird. When I'm getting dressed after my shower, I look at the meteorite—proof that the stars always tell the truth.

Jilly hands me the one book she knows I hate and I read it to her for bedtime like I promised. It's long and even though Jilly falls asleep near the end, I read the whole thing. I turn off her light, close her door, and go to my room.

I find the one tiny meteorite that fell and roll it between my finger and thumb.

"It's going to be our good luck charm," I say to the rock.

"Okay."

"I'm going to keep it in my pocket until this whole mess is over," I say.

I hear the back door close and Mom come in.

"Must be nice to be a meteorite," I say. "You're probably really old and people respect you and stuff."

"You should go and talk to her," the rock says.

"She's probably working late."

"If you stay up here, she won't know that you want to talk to her. But if you go down and tell her, she'll know."

I ask, "What did it feel like to fall from space?"

"Scary," the rock says. "And hot."

That's how I feel when I walk down the stairs to talk to Mom.

....

She's not working late. She's reading a book. This makes me feel even worse because she doesn't get a lot of time to read books.

"It's past ten," she says.

"You okay?" I ask.

"Yeah. Thanks. I'm so sorry I got upset after dinner. I just—it's hard still, sometimes."

I try a few sentences in my head about Tiffany but none of them sound right. It's like the only person I can really talk to around here is the meteorite. I manage, "You always say it's adult-stuff—like we don't know what's going on. But I think I know a lot more than you think I do."

Mom smiles and shakes her head in a way like she knows what I'm talking about.

"I thought you guys had the perfect marriage," I say.

"We did, once. Things change," Mom says.

"I don't understand why Dad changed so much. What happened to him?" I ask.

"Your dad has a lot of guilt, you know. Guilt he can't let go of or can't get ahold of. It kinda ate him up," she says.

I say, "He's such a mess now. It's all fake or something. Like when he took us to that baseball game on the first day we saw him. He ate a hot dog!" I say.

"He struggles a lot," Mom says. "With things that you and I can't understand. It's different for guys I think. I don't know why it's different for them, or if it really is, but I guess it's that whole knight-in-shining-armor thing they have. They think they have to be perfect to save the day. They don't like mistakes. I don't know if it's only boys. But my dad has it. My brother has it. Your dad has it."

"But nobody's perfect," I say.

"Exactly."

"So why be a jerk, then?" I ask. "Why be a jerk instead of perfect? Why not just figure out that nobody is perfect and not be a jerk?"

Mom sits for a while and bites the inside of her mouth. She finally says, "Guilt is probably the most powerful feeling in the world. It really makes a mess of people."

"But if someone is guilty, they should make things right and not do whatever made them guilty again. Like— remember that time I said my room was clean but really I stuffed everything in my closet? Dad told me that lying leads to guilt and he was right! I stopped lying and I felt better," I say.

"Maybe kid guilt and grown-up guilt are different," she says. "I don't know. I'm not him. I do know the minute he let that guilt get a grip on him, he made a lot of decisions without talking to any of us first."

"Like moving Tiffany in and not telling us."

She shakes her head in disappointment. "I just wish he would have told me so I could have prepared you. It must have been weird," she says.

"It was."

"I'm sorry he did that to you," she says.

"I'm sorry he did that to you, too," I say. "All of it."

We hug. I go to bed and think about guilt and mistakes and perfection.

....

The whole reason I had to kick Ethan McGarret in the privates in fourth grade was because I kicked a home run in kickball at recess and his team lost. His team was undefeated until that day.

So he chased me around the field and up the steps and around the sidewalks until I realized that he wasn't going to stop. Until I realized he was actually angry. At me. For kicking a ball. For getting a home run. At recess.

I ran out of breath and hid where the doors to school were. He found me and put his hand on my shoulder—grabbed it hard. His other arm pulled back to punch me and I looked at his face. I kept saying his name before I kicked him. "Ethan! Ethan!" But he was somewhere else.

Now I know the name of that place.

Planet Perfection.

Where every kickball game is won, every answer in class is right, and every person at school wants to be your friend because you're cool.

Planet Perfection doesn't exist.

I don't really feel guilty about misplacing Leah's mom's ring. I know it was wrong. But I had no other choice. The ring was lying there on the floor of the hallway. I could have just given it to Leah, but because she excommunicated me the day before, she would have thought I stole it. I could have given it to a teacher, but I thought I'd get in trouble. So I put it in my pocket until we went to the library a half hour later and I found a place where it would be safe.

Sounds hard to believe. Which is why I never gave the ring back. But now I have to give the ring back. My family depends on it. And I never want to get so guilty that I end up like Dad.

Chapter 39 — Tubas Are Cool

MONDAY, SEPTEMBER 16, 2019

I can't stop thinking about Jilly getting caught. She's so young. I should have never sent her on this mission. I can't even eat my lunch I'm so nervous. My new friend Maya asks if I'm okay. I tell her it's the rain—that it makes me weird. She says that I should never move to Seattle because her dad lived there for a while and he said all it did was rain.

"You're so nice," I say.

"So are you," she answers. But I know I'm not nice. I'm a horrible sister. I touch the little meteorite inside my pocket to make me feel better about it, but it doesn't.

By the time the bus drops me off at the end of our lane, the rain is coming down sideways. Mom is waiting in her car at the bus stop.

"Finn!" she calls out the window. He looks around. "Finn! Let me drive you home!"

Finn gets into the back seat and he's soaked. Mom takes off after the bus and Finn says, "Thanks, Mrs. J."

"How you doing?" Mom asks.

"Okay, I guess." He pushes his wet hair out of his face, but it falls back again.

"How's middle school?" she asks.

"I'm getting used to it," he says.

"Liberty is finally getting used to the schedule. She was so tired at first, weren't you, Lib?"

I'm so nervous, I can't find one word to say to Finn Nolan. All I'm thinking about is Jilly sitting in the chair in front of Ms. S.'s desk, having to explain how I sent her on a mission. She's never been in trouble, not once.

The road is like a shallow river. Mom drives up the hill, turns into the Nolans' driveway, and parks by the front door.

"Thanks again!" Finn says. He seems a lot nicer when Mom is around. I'm probably worrying about him for nothing.

"I'll get Patrick when I pick up Jilly," Mom says. "Go get dry!"

As we drive back to Lou's lane and wait for Jilly's bus to come, I get so nervous about the mission that I feel tingly all over.

"He's a nice kid," Mom says.

"I guess."

"You didn't say anything to him," she says.

"He doesn't really talk to me," I say. "Middle school is awkward."

"I hope they're doing okay," she says. "I worry about those boys."

A tree limb falls onto the road in front of us. We both jump.

Mom gets out of the car, drags the limb to the side of the road, and gets back in, soaked.

Thunder roars.

Jilly's bus comes around the corner and stops. Jilly runs to the car and Mom beeps the horn at Patrick, but he doesn't even look our way. She rolls down the window and yells. As Jilly gets into the car, I give her a look like she shouldn't say anything.

Patrick gets into the car then and thanks Mom for the ride home.

Once we drop Patrick off at his house, Jilly says, "We had an assembly today about instruments. I think I want to play the tuba."

It takes all the willpower I have not to ask how library class was. I say, "Tubas are cool." I feel stupid for saying it. But tubas are cool.

By the time we get back to our house, all of us are soaked and cold and Jilly is crying because the thunder is so loud.

And then the power goes out.

Mom lights candles and pulls out two camping lanterns. We stay together, so I can't ask Jilly about the mission. While we're eating, she must remember it.

She says, "So, because of the assembly, we didn't have any special classes today. Library got moved to Wednesday."

She looks right at me when she says it. Something about her looks so small and innocent, I start to cry. I can't stop myself. And when she sees me cry, she starts, too. The thunder is so loud, it shakes the house. The rain is so heavy, Mom checks to make sure the basement isn't flooding.

I whisper, "Don't worry about the mission anymore, okay?"

"It's fine. I just have to wait 'til Wednesday."

"I don't want to get you in trouble," I say.

"I won't get in trouble," she says.

Lightning touches down in the backyard and lights up the dark house. Thunder rattles the windows. We go to bed early, and all three of us land in Mom's bed because the storm is so scary we can't sleep.

Chapter 40 – Worst Sister Ever

Jilly told me this morning that she's confident that today she will find the item. Part of me wanted to talk her out of it, but part of me really wants to get this over with. I told her she was awesome for doing it. I am still the worst sister ever.

I thought about talking to Mom about it. I thought about making an anonymous email address and sending a letter to Ms. S. so she could go get it herself. I had a bunch of ideas like this. All of them make me a coward.

But now that today is here, I'd rather be a coward than a bad sister.

I don't pay attention to anything in school. Maya says I'm weird at lunch again and I probably am. I don't take any notes in biology class. I keep watching the clocks and the closer it gets to dismissal time, the slower the clocks move.

....

I see Finn Nolan on the bus. He's still quiet. His face is always scrunched up into itself under his uncut bangs. I think maybe he's being his own middle school bodyguard, like the way Dad had Bobby Heffner. I say hi, but he doesn't answer me so I sit in my seat and look out the window. The bus ride is four million hours long.

....

When I get home, Mom has a tent set up in the living room. She's inside the tent, sleeping.

I say, "Hi, Mom." She shifts a little and stays asleep. I go upstairs to my room.

"I'm the worst sister ever," I say to the rock.

"I can't disagree," the rock answers.

"She wanted to do it," I say.

"Sure."

"I'm awful," I say.

"Probably not awful," the rock says. "But you could have done it yourself."

"I know."

I go back downstairs and I wait for Jilly. The clock comes to a standstill. I decide to meet her at the bus stop and I leave a note for Mom if she wakes up while I'm gone.

The frogs are loud and it's funny how I don't hear them when I'm not listening. Birds, too. Jilly says she wants to live in the city one day. On days like this, I can't see myself living anywhere but the country.

Jilly gets off the bus and sees me. As she crosses the road in front of the bus, the first thing she does is give me the thumbs-up. Both hands. Points to her pocket. Then she goes back to pretending like today is any other day. I squeeze the pocket-meteor between my fingers. It feels lucky.

"Where's Mom?"

"Taking a nap," I say. "How did it go?"

"Mission accomplished. We will never speak of it again," she says, and she hands me the ring.

I look down at it in my palm and feel a mix of shame, regret, excitement, and relief. I stop and hug her and pick her up and spin her around. "Thank you!" I say.

"I don't know what you're thanking me for," she says.

"Were you scared?" I ask.

"I don't know what you're talking about." She really meant it when she said we wouldn't speak of it again, I guess.

....

Mom's awake when we get home and she asks Jilly and me to lie down in the tent that's still in the living room. I keep my hand on the pocket where the ring is. I'm afraid it will fall out. I'm afraid Mom will see it.

I finally crawl out of the tent, which Mom deems too small for two real people, and I go to my room.

"I got it back," I say to the rock.

The rock says, "Good for you, I guess."

"Everything is fine. Jilly didn't get caught."

The rock says, "If you think everything is fine, it must be fine."

"I need help. I need to figure out what to do next," I say.

The rock says, "Tell Mom. Go to Leah's house tonight and give it back."

"I was thinking I could drop it in Mike's backpack. Or Finn's! I don't know. It could get them in trouble."

The rock says, "Tell Mom. Go to Leah's house tonight and give it back."

"I could put it in the lost and found at school, but then it could get stolen and I don't want it to get stolen. I could get someone else to leave it in the office. Or I could get them to give it to a teacher and say they found it somewhere."

The rock says, "Tell Mom. Go to Leah's house tonight and give it back."

"You're no help at all," I say.

The rock says, "If you say so."

I put the ring into an envelope. I print out Leah's name on the printer. I tape the name to the envelope. I put the envelope into my backpack front pocket. I take out my Spanish homework and sit at the table.

I feel like calling Dad and asking him if he's ready to come back now.

When I go to bed, I cover the meteorite with a blanket so it doesn't see me.

I know that's irrational, but what's rational when I'm making deals with things that are hundreds and thousands of light-years away?

Part Five:

HOW
TO
BE
POLARIS

Chapter 41 – Waiting and Waiting

THE SLOWEST WEEK EVER

I take the item to school on Thursday morning and slip it into the anti-bullying box outside the guidance office before homeroom. I stand across the hall for a minute to make sure no one saw me, and then I go to my locker.

By biology class, I hear that Leah got her ring back.

That's it.

The whole thing is over.

I expected to feel a huge weight lift, but I don't. I try to imagine life with Dad back at home. I have trouble imagining it because all I can remember are the bad times. I try to picture the family of deer. Holding his hand.

The weight still doesn't lift.

....

The weekend is relaxing. Jilly and I sleep past ten on Saturday. Mom got a few new movies on DVD and we hang around in our pajamas and eat popcorn and watch them. We make pizza Sunday night and have a picnic on the living room floor.

Monday, I have my hopes up for a phone call from Dad. I don't know why. The stars had all weekend to fix things. Leah has her dumb ring back. Dad doesn't call.

Tuesday, I forget all about Dad until he calls during dinner and he and Mom have a talk about something in code. I hope the code is that they love each other again and he's moving back in.

On Wednesday, we have another storm like last week. Lou comes to the house to double-check if the basement is dry and to give Mom some meat. Sounds weird, but Lou doesn't just hang the heads on his wall when he hunts. He makes food, too.

"Elk!" Mom says, digging through a cooler that's in the bed of Lou's truck. "I love elk!"

Jilly makes a face like she'd never eat elk in her life.

"You eat elk, Jilly. You just don't know it," Mom says.

Lou leaves some kind of pump in the basement just in case. "It's gonna be windy with lightning. If you lose power, call me. I have the generator ready."

Lou clearly doesn't understand Mom at all. She could live without electricity indefinitely. She likes it that way. "Bring on the zombie apocalypse!" she says, flexing her arms. Lou laughs and gets back in his truck.

The storm is worse than last week's. It's a leftover hurricane. The lightning is scary and the thunder is loud. Jilly and I sleep in Mom's bed again.

....

We never really recover from Wednesday. I'm tired and Jilly is cranky. Or maybe Jilly is tired and I'm cranky. I can't shift my mood. I know why, but I don't say why because it's a stupid reason why. Thursday I try to daydream Tiffany moving out of Dad's new house. I see them argue and I see her packing her WELL-BEHAVED WOMEN RARELY MAKE HISTORY mug into the trunk of her car. I see Dad sitting in his darkened bedroom, lonely and ready to finally just come home. By the time I get back from school, I expect to see him there.

He's not there.

Thursday night I go out to talk to the stars. The hill is muddy so I don't even sit down. My arms are crossed. I tilt my head back and ask, "Okay, when are you gonna deliver on your promise?"

I look for my answer.

I see three things: a canoe, a rabbit, and an ice cream cone.

I try to make the rabbit into Dad. I try to make the ice cream cone into Mom. I try to make them hold hands and go for a walk, or get into the canoe and enjoy a trip down the river. None of this makes sense. Rabbits and ice cream cones do not belong together—not inside or outside a canoe.

Chapter 42 — The Day My Brain Ate My Brain

Dad picks us up for our weekend with him and talks super fast in the car on the way to his house. He has plans. Dad always has plans now.

"Tonight we're going to a movie and then tomorrow it's out to the lake to canoe and get some exercise!"

"We exercise all the time," I say.

"I just meant canoeing. You love canoeing!"

Jilly is quiet and tired. "As long as we don't go fishing," she says.

Dad puts an animated frown on his face. "Aw, Jilly. Fishing is fun. Gets you out into the fresh air."

"Gets the fish out into the fresh air, too. And then they die," Jilly says.

"And then Sunday, Tiff and I have something really special planned," he says.

"Maybe we could just hang out at your house this weekend in our pajamas," I say. "We could watch TV or movies and make food and just be together."

"Oh," he says.

"I'd like that," Jilly says.

Dad goes quiet. We park outside his town house and Dad gets both of our backpacks from the trunk of his car and I wait for him to hand me mine, but he walks inside and puts them on the couch. Jilly is dragging her feet. We get inside the door and stand there.

"So what do you want to do now?" he asks.

"We just got here," I say.

"I want to take a nap," Jilly says.

"Lazybones!" Dad says. He's trying to be funny. Jilly doesn't take it that way and storms upstairs and closes the door to our bedroom. "She okay?" he asks me.

"She's tired. Long week at school and she was up late the other night because of the storm."

"Still scared of thunder, huh?"

"She's ten," I say.

"Maybe if she gets a nap now, she'll be more excited about the weekend's plans," he says.

"We're tired and we just want to relax," I say.

"Oh," he says. "Sorry. I'm just trying to be a good dad."

"You are a good dad. But we can't always be going on adventures. It's just a weekend to us, you know? You don't have to entertain us."

"Okay," he says. He walks to the kitchen table and opens his laptop.

Eventually, I sit down on the couch. I don't throw myself at it the way I would at home. I don't curl up and cuddle the nearest pillow. I just sit. Like I'm in a doctor's office waiting room. My mind moves faster, not slower. I don't relax. I can't relax.

I take a few deep breaths and they help. I pull out my sketchbook and a pencil from my backpack and I lie down and take up half the couch. I try to figure out what I want to draw or write in the book but my mind is unreasonably fast.

I take more deep breaths and close my eyes. I can't figure out how to relax. I think about how this could mean something is wrong with me. Like on the websites I read. Racing thoughts. Can't stop them. Feeling bad about myself. I can't stop my brain.

I'm a good kid. I do good kid things.

So why did I put Jilly in danger?

I didn't really put her in danger. I'm a good kid.

If I was a good kid, Dad would be talking to me and not working on his computer.

Dad just wants you to do what he wants to do.

A good kid would just do it.

Jilly was tired. I just wanted to be a good sister.

Mom doesn't mind when we say we want to stay in our pajamas all weekend.

Dad thinks it means we're lazy.

I'm a lazy, bad kid.

For not wanting to go out on the lake in canoes.

He's probably just doing a few little things. He'll probably come and talk to you when he's done.

You're a good kid, Liberty.

"Not you, too!" Dad says this and only when he says it do I realize I wasn't all the way awake.

I open my eyes. He's standing between the kitchen and the living room and he's got his arms crossed. Nothing wrong with that except that he looks mad. Even though he's smiling, he looks mad.

"Sorry," I say.

"Is everything okay?" he asks. He sits on the edge of the couch. This shifts my balance and I have to sit up.

"Everything is fine, Dad. It's just Friday and I'm a little tired, I guess."

"What do they do to you in school that you're so tired?"

I shrug. I don't like the question. They don't do anything to us in school that isn't what they did to him when he was in school.

They wake us up too early.

They give us too much homework.

They bore us with worksheets.

They make us sit for too long.

I miss recess.

I don't say any of those things to Dad.

"How about a cup of coffee?"

I twist up my face like he's weird. I think he's joking. But he's staring at me like he wants an answer. "I don't drink coffee. I'm twelve."

"What would wake you up, then?"

A nap would wake me up.

Or maybe it would make me more tired.

I don't really care.

Why does he keep asking so many questions?

Why is New Dad so weird about normal kid things?

Was Old Dad the same?

If I'm tired outside of bedtime, does that mean I'm depressed?

Did I get it?

How long will I have it?

Why do I feel wrong all the time?

Like I should be someone else?

I am my Liberty.

New Liberty.

Doesn't draw star maps.

Doesn't draw on walls, either.

Doesn't have anyone to talk to. Except the rock.

Exciting exceptions.

I talk to a rock.

The rock says I'm fine.

"Come on. Let's do jumping jacks," Dad says. He starts doing jumping jacks.

That's when Tiffany comes home from work.

Dad stops doing jumping jacks and arranges his hair with his hands. Greets her at the door. A kiss. A hug. She looks at him in a way like he's a puzzle.

She sees it, too.

Liberty Johansen, you are not going irrational.

Dad says, "Don't know what happened to the girls this week in school, but they can't seem to find their energy."

Tiffany smiles at me and waves. I wave back and my hand even looks tired.

"I was telling them about our plans," he says.

"Your plans, Jack," she says. "No offense to the lake, but if the girls want to chill out, I say we chill out. We can make cookies and watch TV." She looks at me. "Sound good?"

I nod.

"Not you, too!" he says.

She hugs him and they laugh together but his laugh is nervous.

"How about pizza for dinner?" Tiffany says.

"Jilly wants sausage," I say.

"What about you?" Tiffany asks.

"I was gonna take them out to that burger place," Dad says.

"We can get pizza delivered. Let's do that instead," Tiffany says.

Dad looks defeated. Over pizza.

But by the time the pizza comes and we're eating off paper plates in the living room while watching Jilly's favorite episode of her favorite cartoon, Dad seems normal again.

This will be the first normal weekend we've had with him since he left.

I'm looking forward to it.

But deep inside I know something is wrong. With him. With me, maybe. With the feeling of relief I had when Tiffany came home and when the pizza came.

Dad isn't happy.
I did something wrong.
I always feel like I did something wrong.
This probably has to do with the item.
I wonder what Dad's item is.
And then I look at Tiffany.

Chapter 43 — Liberty Johansen Is Totally Irrational

I'm irrational. I hate everyone.

I thought I liked Tiffany when she came home but now she's holding Dad's hand and she keeps rubbing it with her thumb and I hate her thumb and her and her floofy flats with bows.

Jilly is clueless. To the thumb-rubbing and to me hating everyone. She's just so okay with all of this and I know she's following my lead so I can't be anything but okay with this but I'm not okay with this. I'm tired of being a broom.

"I'm going to bed," I say.

Because what else is there to do when you suddenly hate everyone?

In bed, I whisper to the tiny meteorite in my pocket and I think about how much I hate Mom.

She could have been better at being a wife. She could have been better at being a mom. She could have been better at scooping ice cream or wearing shoes that didn't look like she was hiking all the time. I don't know. I don't understand any of these thoughts. I told you — I'm irrational.

This isn't like when I threw the toaster through the window. This is new.

I sleep. I don't even hear Jilly come to bed. When I wake

up, it's light out and the house is quiet except for Jilly's breathing.

I look at the clock in the bathroom and see it's six in the morning. I think about walking back to Mom's house. The meteorite is there. I want someone to talk to.

I go downstairs and turn on the TV. I open the book I'm supposed to be reading for English and I stare at the markings on the page. Letters that make words. Like stars that make constellations. We have so many languages, but only one set of accepted constellations. Even in other languages. Ursa Minor is *Osa Menor* in Spanish. *La Petite Ourse* in French. *Orsa Minore* in Italian. *Ursa Mdogo* in Swahili.

It makes no sense. But it's not my business anymore. Someone else can change the way the world sees the night sky in whatever language they want.

Jilly comes down and plops on the couch next to me. "You're up early," she says.

"I guess."

"Went to bed early," she says.

I nod. Jilly's in a mood. This can sometimes scare me but her hair is standing out from her head perfectly horizontal. She looks like a grumpy clown.

"Dad said we can't just sit around all day," she says. "We have to do something. So I told him he could go canoeing with Tiffany if he wanted and you'd babysit."

"Sounds good to me."

"He said it's not him who needs to get out, it's us," she says.

I wonder if Tiffany can just sit on the couch in her pajamas on weekends or if when we're not here, he makes her climb rocks or something.

I'm exhausted and it's not even seven in the morning.

"If Dad asks," I say, "tell him I went for a walk."

I get up, put my shoes on, and walk out the front door.

....

There's a farmer's market on Saturdays and I think about wandering through and cooling off. I don't know why I'm so hot inside. It's not like a fever. It's not like anything else that's hot.

The farmer's market doesn't open for another hour, so I keep walking. An old man in a car waves at me as if he recognizes me. I wave back because I don't want to make him feel bad. I walk to the main street in town and run across it after looking for cars both ways ten times. I'd rather live in the woods by myself. In one of Lou's tree stands, maybe. I don't need much room. No traffic. No streets to cross.

I start walking up the hill to Mom's house. It's a dangerous road—more dangerous than the main street. Once I get up the hill, I avoid the twisty part where there's nowhere to walk and I take a left on the road that overlooks three farms.

Birds are all I hear.

There's a red-tailed hawk circling a field. There's a flock of starlings chirping in a cornfield that's been plowed. There's a woodpecker.

Rather than walk on the road, I cut into Lou's woods as soon as I can.

Only once I get close to Mom's house do I think about Dad waking up and me being gone. I don't know what to feel about that. I can't hang around in my pajamas at his house. I always have to be getting out and doing something.

Well, here I am. I got out and did something.

Chapter 44 — Pajamas Are Everything

It's nine o'clock on a Saturday morning and Mom's car isn't here. I imagine her somewhere quiet, cooking eggs on a fire by herself, reading a book at the same time. I find the key to the back door where we always keep it, and let myself in.

The cabin smells weird when no one is in it. Smells like a mix of hamster cage and damp. Sounds gross, but that's what it smells like. I stop by the fridge and get myself some orange juice. When I see food, I realize I just walked three miles and I'm hungry.

Cereal. Milk. I go upstairs to talk to the rock.

I say, "It must be weird to fall from space only to land here."

Rock says, "What's so wrong with here?"

"I don't even know where I'm supposed to live anymore."

I know I once called Leah Jones the B-word but I'm not someone who curses. I hear curses on the bus and in school and I don't like them. But right now I want to curse out the rock.

I say, "&*&% *%#$&%^$$%!!"

The rock doesn't answer.

I say, "$#@ &%^* %#@*!"

The rock says, "Get it all out, Liberty."

I deflate. I tell the rock I hate it.

The rock tells me it loves me.

This is all so confusing.

....

I decide to take a shower. Showers always help. In the shower I think about how if I don't know where home is, I never will because I'm really from somewhere else. But then I realize that I'm human and I'm most likely from Earth and I'm in middle school and I'm smart enough to know what's really going on.

I just hate everybody.

That's all. No big deal.

"Lib? Is that you?"

I say, "Random strangers take showers in your house?"

Mom says, "Geez, kid. You scared the pants off me."

And then I cry because the shower is a safe place to cry because everything is wet and I have all the time in the world. Or at least until the hot water runs out.

I think it takes about twenty minutes for the hot water to run out. I'm still crying and I don't know what's wrong with me. I feel bad for leaving Jilly at Dad's house. I forgot about that until right now. But then I think Dad and Jilly and Tiffany are probably out running a marathon or kayaking rapids or climbing Mount Kilimanjaro and are having a great time without me.

I just wanted to hang around in my pajamas.

So I go up to my room and put on my pajamas.

Mom calls, "Are you coming down soon?"

I ask the rock. "Am I coming down soon?"

The rock says, "Only if you can hang around in your pajamas."

Mom says, "Sounds like we need to talk."

I go to the closet and pull out my star maps from last winter. The ones that never connected any dots. I look at the first one and I just see dots. Same with the second and third one. Three maps with no connections. That's how I feel.

I'm a map for Jilly with no connections. I'm a map for Mom with no connections. I'm a map for Dad with no connections. I'm useless to all three of them.

The rock says, "You sound depressed."

I yell at the rock. "@%$^*&#!"

"Lib? Can I come up?"

I don't know why she asked. She's already halfway up the attic steps.

I must look worse than I thought. She sighs and her shoulders slump. I try to see myself from where she is. I'm on my bed, maps out in front of me, my hair is soaking wet, and I'm wearing pajamas. Seems like a normal enough Saturday.

"Does Dad know you're here?" she asks.

"Probably not," I say.

"Oh, kiddo. That's not good."

"He's probably off doing something fun," I say. "Probably not worried at all."

"I have to call him," she says.

"NO!" I say this louder than I mean to.

"Liberty. Please."

"If you call him, he'll be angry," I say.

"If you ran away, then he's probably worried. Not angry."

"I didn't run away. I just took a walk and ended up here," I say.

She gets her phone and sends a short text. I don't see what it says but it was short enough to only say *Liberty is here*. "Did you have a bad night? Is that why you . . . took a walk?"

"I just wanted to hang out in my house in my pajamas," I say. "Is that really so bad? To want to have a weekend off to hang around in pajamas and watch TV? Or read a book? It's not that bad, right?"

"What did he want to do?"

"Everything. Raft the Amazon rapids, climb Mount Everest only using one foot."

"Your dad and his plans," she says.

"He's irrational," I say. "I wish I never had to see him again."

"Don't say that."

"Why do you always stick up for him? What did he ever do for you? Look at what he did to us!" I say. "He didn't even see us for eighty-six days after he left. Now he wants to act like he always wanted us around so he looks good for Tiffany. That's all. He doesn't want us to come there and he can't wait for us to leave."

"You really think that?"

"Well why else would he always have to run a mini day camp when we come over? I just wanted to hang out and relax. We're tired. It's the weekend. Jilly took a nap the minute she got there. Not the best time for skiing the Alps, you know?"

"Your sporting geography knowledge is impressive," Mom says. She smiles.

I laugh because she knows just the right time to tell a joke.

"I'm worried about you, Liberty," she says.

I stop laughing.

She says, "You have a lot of stuff going on. Starting middle school. New friends. New everything. And this is all new, too."

"I hated everyone last night. And this morning. Even you." I say this and I don't even cry. Something is wrong with me. I don't hate Mom but I just told her I hate her.

"That's normal."

I say, "That doesn't help."

She nods.

"Everything I do is wrong," I say. "When I'm with Dad I don't even feel like I can breathe right. Or eat right. He always makes a big deal if I get a grilled cheese sandwich and then Tiffany got one and he was fine." Mom is quiet. Listening. "He always loved Jilly more anyway because Jilly is perfect and still little and he doesn't like me because he thinks I'm a *tween*. But really he just wants to have a fast, excitement-filled weekend so he can deal with us being there."

Mom says, "But it's not because he doesn't like *you*. It's because he wants *you* to like *him*. I know that's hard to understand at the moment but think about it a while."

"As long as I can stay here until Sunday," I say. "I'm a kid. He's an adult. He should be the one thinking about it for a while."

"You can stay another hour at most. But then I have to take you back to your dad's house." She sees my face and adds, "Jilly must already miss you."

Her phone dings with a text and she ignores it.

"I didn't really hate you," I say. "I'm just so hot inside. I thought about living in one of Lou's tree stands."

"Not a lot of room up there to sleep. First step is a doozy," she says. She points to my star maps. "Are you getting back into your old habits? I hope so."

I hold up her map. "You can have this one. Maybe you can connect the dots. I can't."

"What? No. That's your thing. Not my thing."

"I can't do any new ones until these are done. And I can't figure them out," I say.

"Why not?"

"My hands are brooms," I say. I hold up my hands.

Mom looks at me like she's making the appointment with Jan in her head right this very minute. "Okay," she says.

"Just connect the dots the way you see them," I say.

She walks toward the door with the star map under her elbow. Smiles. Says, "Stay in your pajamas and I'll run you back to Dad's in a half hour. Sound good?"

I'm not sure why, but yes, it sounds good.

Chapter 45 — All for Nothing

"When you said everything you do is wrong earlier, what did you mean?" Mom asks on the way to Dad's house. I think her timing isn't the best. I don't want to walk into Dad's crying.

"I just feel like everything is my fault or something," I say.

"Like the divorce?" she asks. "Because if it's the divorce and you want to talk about it, I can."

"I don't want to make you upset," I say.

"I don't care if you make me upset. And I don't think you will. I probably haven't done a great job of talking to you about it because it was hard there for a long time."

"It's not hard anymore?"

She takes a deep breath as if she's asking herself. "Not as bad as before, no. Rosemary has helped me a lot. It's a process, like grief."

"Oh."

"Ask me anything." She pulls the car over and parks on the side of the street.

I sit for a minute trying to think of the most important questions.

"Okay," I say. "This is what I think happened. I think Dad wasn't a great husband for a long time because he had depression and he didn't know it. Right?"

"Something like that," she says.

"And then once he found out, he felt bad."

"He didn't like taking medication and he didn't like knowing that he wasn't perfect, I think," Mom says.

"So what—he . . ." I stop because this feels like adult-stuff. It *is* adult-stuff. I suddenly want no part in adult-stuff. "Um . . . he found a girlfriend? While he was still married to you? Because he wasn't perfect?"

"Uhh," Mom says.

"It's okay. You don't have to answer that," I say. I really don't want to know any adult-stuff ever again.

Mom makes that face where her lips curl in and she's grimacing a bit. "As silly as that sounds, your guess is about right."

"Even though Jilly and I were born and we were having a good family life and all that?" I ask. "He just went and got a girlfriend."

"You'll have to ask him how he did it. The whole point was that I didn't know," she says. "And don't think too badly of him. We had a great marriage for a long time. This girlfriend stuff is a lot more common than you think."

"It's gross," I say.

"It is what it is."

"Gross."

"Yeah. It's gross."

I hesitate. "I . . . uh . . . did you do it, too?"

"Nah. Not my style," she says.

"Did you ever feel like everything you did was wrong?" I ask.

"Since Dad moved out, all the time. But now I know it was the right thing to do. I mean, now that he's happy with Tiffany, I'm glad we decided to separate."

"I don't think he's happy with Tiffany," I say.

"Well if he's not, then that's his problem."

"How can you say that? He's Dad!"

"His problems aren't my problems anymore. Unless they involve you guys. His problems are his problems," she says. "I tried a long time to help him. In the end, Dad made some choices that I couldn't help him with. And here we are."

"Did Dad think he was wrong about everything once?"

"Yes."

"We always said that I was like him and Jilly was like you. Should I be worried I'm going to act like him when I'm older?"

"No. Because you're not the same person. You're you. He's him. You have support now, so if you have thoughts like his, we can work on them early. He didn't have that. You're you. He's him. And while we all have things in common, the choices we make are ours."

"He cheated on you!"

"Right."

"That's a horrible choice!" I say.

"It is. But he had some sort of master plan. Inside his head. Secrets," she says. "Just remember—the more open and honest you are, the better your life will be. With or without depression. Depression shuts people up. That's one of the ways it's dangerous."

I was shut up since I misplaced Leah's mom's ring and didn't feel guilty about it. Maybe longer. I haven't told anyone anything for real since January. Just the rock.

I say, "Can we go back to the house? I forgot something."

She turns the car around in a parking lot and we head back up the hill. The whole way, I consider telling her about the ring. It's my secret. It's probably the thing that's making me so hot all the time. And now—now I know that even if the stars keep their side of the deal, Mom and Dad don't want to be together.

I feel so immature.

I wasted the whole month wishing for something impossible. Like when Jilly asked for a hedgehog even though she knew she couldn't get it.

But this is different. Jilly was happy when she got a hamster instead. I haven't thought about being happy with what I got. I haven't really even thought about what I got. A mom in one house. A dad in another. I haven't really thought about that since the week we fell from space. I just felt like I was still falling the whole time.

When we get to the cabin, I go inside, get my backpack, and roll the meteorite into it. Still can't believe how heavy it is. Still can't believe a meteorite fell to Earth while I was sitting right there. But it did. Some things are impossible to believe but they happen anyway. Like my dad cheating on my mom because he felt like he should be perfect. Like me picking up the ring off the hallway floor and not giving it to a teacher because I was afraid of what Leah would say. Doesn't make any sense. But maybe that's what fear does. It makes us do weird things that make sense in the moment, but make no sense from nine months away.

Maybe, from where Polaris is, 433 light-years away, all of this makes sense.

When I get back into the car, Mom asks what's in the backpack.

"A meteorite."

"Looks big," she says. She's saying it like there's no meteorite in my backpack.

"It's not that big, but it's heavy because it's got metal in it."

Mom looks puzzled. "You're serious, aren't you?"

"Yup."

"Was it from that night when the windows broke?"

"The rock is sorry it broke your windows and I'm sorry I broke your windows. We have a lot in common."

We stay quiet until we get to Dad's house.

I'm still in my pajamas.

Chapter 46 – The Day I Crushed My Dad

"How could you just walk away like that?"

That's Dad. He doesn't notice that I have a 130-pound backpack on my back. I scoot past him as he's talking in his serious-Dad voice so I can sit on the couch and coax the shoulder straps off my arms.

"We were worried!

"You have to think about us, too!"

Jilly is sitting at the kitchen table. She's rolling the edge of Tiffany's tablecloth between her fingers and she looks like she wants to cry. I hope she doesn't hold back. I hope she cries and Dad stops paying attention to me.

"You can't be so selfish!" he says.

I'm not sure what's happening to me. I ask the rock. Brain-to-rock-brain. The rock can't tell me what's happening. Next thing I know, I'm hot as daytime on Mercury and words are coming out of my mouth.

Loud.

"Selfish? You cheated on Mom. You're selfish!"

Dad looks at Jilly. He looks back at me. He looks at Tiffany, who's doing a great job of counting the lines in her palms over in the chair. He says to Tiffany, "I need a minute with you."

"I'm right here, Dad. You can't listen to me when I'm finally telling you my feelings? Seems pretty selfish to me!"

Dad goes upstairs with Tiffany. I pace the living room and end up at the kitchen table with Jilly.

"You okay?" I ask.

She says, "He said it was my fault for letting you leave."

This makes me hotter than I already was.

I hear Tiffany talking to Dad in their bedroom. I can only hear the low murmur of conversation, not actual words. He isn't saying anything. Jilly starts to cry.

"He cheated on Mom?" she asks.

I nod. I feel so guilty. She probably shouldn't know this stuff so young.

"Did she tell you this?"

"I asked her," I say. "She answered."

"You brought the meteorite," she says, and points to the backpack on the couch.

"I don't even know why, now."

"Were you going to show it to him? And some maps?" she asks.

I look at the couch. That's what it looks like. It looks like I brought all the things that matter to me for some kind of show-and-tell.

"Mom said he'd be happy to see me and that he'd understand."

"He was worried," Jilly says.

"Well then he should have been happy to see me," I say, grabbing one of the two maps and handing it to Jilly. "That's your map now. You have to find what you see in there and draw it in."

"I don't make maps," Jilly says.

"Just this one. Connect the dots for me."

She unrolls her map on the kitchen floor and looks at it from every angle. Squints. Sighs. She gets a pencil and sits next to it. I sit on the couch next to the meteorite.

By the time I'm called upstairs to talk, I'm angrier than I was before I walked in. I have so many questions.

"Can't you see why I left this morning? Can't you see how hard this whole year has been? Can't you see what you did to me and Jilly? Can't you feel bad for just one second about what you did to Mom?"

Tiffany is downstairs with Jilly. It's just me and Dad. And these questions.

"I feel awful about what I did to Mom," he says.

I stay quiet.

"I feel awful for what I did to our family," he says. "But I don't know what that has to do with you walking to Mom's this morning. That's dangerous. You can't do that again."

"Well I can't climb Mount Everest every other week-end. And neither can Jilly. We just want to have weekends off like normal kids."

"You could have just told me," he says.

"You don't listen," I say.

We're quiet for a minute. It's tense quiet, not forest-silent-walk quiet.

"Your mom texted to say she told you about what really happened," he says.

"I already knew, Dad. The first time we came here you had a glass by the sink with lipstick on it."

He looks ashamed. He should.

"And that time you came to drop off my strep throat medicine and had a woman hiding in the car. Do you remember that? Jilly and I both watched when she sat up."

"You were spying on me?" he says.

"No. We loved you and you were our father and we missed you and would watch you drive away. We didn't know there was a woman in the car until she sat up. You laughed the whole time. Is it funny now?"

He puts his face in his hands.

"And what about us? You didn't see us for three months after you left. You kept saying you would and then you'd cancel. You told us you'd try and you'd come back and the family would maybe work out," I say. "You just lied."

He says, "Stop."

I don't stop.

I tell him that we needed him. I tell him that we loved him. I tell him that we're trying. "Look at how we treated Tiffany the night we first met her. We were nice! And then suddenly you don't even tell us that she's living here and we were still nice!"

He can't pull his face out from behind his hands.

I try to find any part of me that isn't hot. Everything is hot.

"If you cared about us at all, you'd have told us what was going on," I say. "You'd explain it to us. Try to help us understand why you decided that Mom and Jilly and me weren't enough to make you happy. But I don't think you're happy. Not even now with your new girlfriend and your fancy single life. I don't think you'll ever be happy." I didn't curse once but I feel like everything I just said was a curse word.

He's still sitting there with his head in his hands.

I don't have time for this.

I get up and leave the room and slam the door.

I go downstairs and I feel trapped. Tiffany is on the floor with Jilly squinting at the map.

Jilly says, "We heard all that, you know."

Tiffany says, "You have every reason to be mad."

I say, "I can't stay here."

Jilly says, "My stomach hurts."

Tiffany starts to cry.

She was the last person I expected to cry. I thought maybe Dad would and Jilly, of course. Or even me.

Now I feel horrible.

Chapter 47 — Meteorites Don't Eat Hamburgers II

We're at Burger King. It's dark out, so it's got to be past eight o'clock. Dad's eyes are red and they look small on his face. Tiffany is eating her french fries one by one and doesn't seem to be chewing them.

Jilly is pretending the toy she got with her kids' meal is interesting but it's really just plastic junk.

I say, "This is depressing."

No one answers. So I take a bite of my hamburger.

Fast food is gross.

I don't think I'll ever be able to eat at Burger King again.

....

We had a family meeting because Tiffany was crying. Dad said that it wasn't fair of me to make Tiffany cry. Tiffany said that I didn't make her cry. Dad didn't listen to her until she cried more.

Dad and Tiffany went back upstairs to work things out. Jilly and I watched TV. I don't even remember what we watched and it was only a few hours ago. Then, when Dad and Tiffany came downstairs, he said we were going out to eat. He was in sweatpants. We came to Burger King.

When we get back to his house, Jilly looks so tired. I feel tired but also super awake. The meteorite is still in my backpack on the couch. Tiffany pours herself a glass of wine. Dad sits at the kitchen table with a piece of blank paper in front of him but no pencil.

Jilly goes to my backpack and opens the zipper.

I don't stop her. I do say, "Be careful," because if the rock rolls out, it could fall and break her foot.

I help her get it out of the backpack and we prop it up with pillows.

Tiffany asks, "What's that?"

I say, "A meteorite."

She looks at it, and then me, and then she walks over to the couch. "Like, from space?"

Jilly says, "Yep. All the way from space."

"Are you serious? Jack. Are they serious?"

Dad has found a pencil and is writing something on the piece of paper in front of him.

"I saw it fall," I say. "Pretty amazing."

The rock says, "You asked for change. I brought you change."

I look at Tiffany. I look at Jilly.

No one else hears the rock.

"It's just a rock, right?" Tiffany says. "It's not really from space. Right? Can rocks even fall from space?"

I say, "Stuff falls from space all the time. Well, not *all* the time. That would be weird. But yeah. This rock was a meteor and then it got through the atmosphere."

"You were there?" Tiffany's eyes are big, like I'm telling her a secret.

"The boom broke the windows!" Jilly says.

"I have something for you," Dad says. I didn't even hear him get up. Sometimes when he's really sad, he moves around and makes no noise at all. He hands me the paper. I go to read it but he tells me to read it when I'm by myself. I stuff it into the pocket of my pajamas and I reach onto the couch and hand him the last no-connection star map.

"The dots are there," I say. "But I can't connect them."

He blinks a few times and looks at me, concerned. He takes the map to the kitchen table and opens it. Tiffany goes to look as if he's just opened a treasure map. The two of them stare at it and Dad asks, "When's this from?"

"The week of January eighteenth to the twenty-fifth," I say.

"How do you even remember that?" Tiffany asks.

Dad says, "It's the week I moved out."

"The week we fell from space," I say.

Chapter 48 — Lost Luggage

SUNDAY, SEPTEMBER 29, 2019

Dear Liberty,

You're right about how I lied to you. You're right about how I hurt our family. You're right about how I hurt Mom. Most of all, you're right about how I'm not happy. Not even now.

You girls were so kind to Tiffany when you met her. You're probably kinder to her than I've been to her. Sometimes I can't keep up with myself. I'm so sorry for how I treated you after I moved out. I wasn't okay enough to be a father. I'm not sure I've ever been okay enough to be a father. But I'm ready to try now.

You're so smart and talented. I remember when you set out to change the world. Do you remember the night you told us about your new constellations? Mom says you aren't drawing maps anymore and I know that's my fault.

I want to find a way to help you get back to where you were. Liberty, I love you. I just want to help you *get through this time so you can do everything you want to do.*

> Love,
> Dad

I read it twice, once I get to bed. I try not to be angry, but I'm still angry. I think about the night I first told Mom and Dad about the new constellations and I feel stupid.

I think back to the silent walks Dad and I used to take. Sometimes we'd walk only half a mile in three hours. Not a word between us. It was special.

I'm mad that he can't remember how special that was. I'm sad that he thinks he wasn't ever a good dad. He was a great dad. That's what I fall asleep thinking about. How he was a great dad.

....

When I go downstairs for breakfast, the three of them, Jilly, Dad, and Tiffany, are sitting around the kitchen table— tablecloth off, pencils in hand, still in their pajamas— looking at the two star maps I gave to them. Dad is brewing coffee and Jilly has cream cheese on her chin so I know she just ate a bagel.

"Is there a sesame bagel left for me?" I ask.

"Already sliced and waiting," Dad says, not taking his eyes off the map.

My favorite bagel, ready in the toaster. I push the lever down and wait.

Jilly is in deep concentration over her map. Her eyebrows are bent down into the space above her nose.

Tiffany is looking at her phone. She says, "I can't understand how you draw all these in the right places." She shows me the phone. It's a picture of the night sky.

I shrug. The toaster shrugs—and my bagel arrives, toasted.

There's no room on the kitchen table for me or my bagel so I fix it and eat it at the counter. None of them are talking to me. They're all squinting at the dots. Same as I did for months until I ripped them down.

I finish my bagel and sit on the couch.

"I think this looks like a sled," Tiffany says.

"I think it looks like a horse," Jilly says. "Lying down."

I want to tell them that they're doing it wrong, but I don't.

The rock is still propped up by pillows. It doesn't say anything. Not even when I stare at it.

"Liberty, this is a horse, right?" Jilly says.

I stay quiet. I hope Dad will tell her that she has to figure it out herself.

He doesn't.

She says, "Right?"

"I can't tell you what you see. Only you can see what you see," I say.

"But it's your map!" Jilly says.

"I gave them to you guys. They're yours now."

Tiffany says, "You're not going to stop making them, are you?"

Jilly says, "She already did."

Dad deflates a little. Maybe he's finally seeing outside of his own head.

....

It's Sunday afternoon. The star maps are still out on the kitchen table. Jilly and Tiffany have gone to the store for dinner ingredients. Dad is still staring at the dots on his map. He stands on the kitchen chair and looks down at the map and smiles.

"Got it!" he says.

He sits down and draws a bunch of lines. I can't see what he's drawing from where I'm sitting on the couch, so I get up.

He holds his hand up for me to stop. "Let me draw it first."

He draws. It feels like an hour but it's probably three minutes. He draws the lines in lightly at first, then makes them heavier once he's confident. He keeps saying, "Wow."

When he finally calls me over to see it, I try to smile but I can't make my mouth smile because my lip is quivering too much.

It's a drawing of a buck. Our buck. Just his face and antlers huge in the sky. Dad didn't even have to make up any fake stars. They connected this way naturally.

He stands there wanting some sort of reaction and all I feel is sad.

"What's wrong?" he asks.

I want to tell him how I'm feeling, but all I'm feeling is mixed up. I shake my head.

"Lib, what's wrong?"

"I think I could have what you have," I say. I'm crying.

"You mean depression?" Dad asks.

I nod and cry.

"It's going to be okay."

"I don't want Mom to know," I say.

"Why not?"

"I don't want her to have to live with me like this after having to live with you like this," I say.

"Your mom is the strongest woman I know," he says.

"She's going through a divorce! And her husband is living with his girlfriend!"

"True," he says. "But I know your mother. She'd want to know if you're feeling these things."

"I threw a toaster through the window," I say. "It was a while ago, but I think she knows I'm feeling like this, I guess. But not this bad."

Dad doesn't know what to say to this. He puts down the pencil and leaves the buck in the night sky in January and sits on the couch and makes me sit next to him. The whole time, the meteorite is there, making me tell the truth.

"Can you explain the feeling?" he asks.

"I'm just . . . not happy."

"Like, sad all the time or just not happy? Do you think about—um—do you think about bad things?"

I think about this question. Yes, I think about bad

things because I live in a bad thing. Divorce is a bad thing. How do I answer a question like this? "How do you feel about being in the middle of a divorce?" I ask.

"It's horrible," he says.

"Exactly."

"So that's the bad thing you think about?"

I nod.

"I wish I could go back in time, Lib," he says.

"Do you?"

"I don't know. I mean, yes and no. It's a lot of stuff you wouldn't understand yet. Like—maybe I married your mom because she was so strong. Maybe I wanted her to save me from all this stuff."

"And then you left," I say.

He's quiet for a few seconds. "I want to talk about you. I want to know why you're not happy. If you can see a reason, if it's situational, you know? And not something more lasting," he says.

I don't know if there was a question in there anywhere.

I also don't know why I'm not happy. But nobody ever asks me that.

"I do," the rock says from behind me. "I ask you all the time."

I try to figure out what to say. I can't figure it out. First I want to tell him my hands are brooms, but that makes no sense. Then I want to tell him about Leah's mom's ring. Even though the whole thing is over. I don't understand why it's bugging me so much because I never even felt that bad about it. Then I think about how dumb I was to think Mom and Dad could get back together. I say, "I don't want to talk about this anymore."

Dad shrinks.

"Tell him about me," the rock says.

"I'm sure you saw that," I say, pointing to the meteorite.

"Big rock," he says.

Dad isn't paying full attention. He looks panicked. "I want to talk about you and how we can help."

"It's a meteorite," I say.

"We'll see the doctor as soon as we can and Mom says that you like that therapist you've been talking to."

"It's a meteorite," I say again.

He stops and looks at the rock. Looks back at me.

"I'm serious. I watched it fall," I say.

Dad tries to pick up the meteorite like it's some regular rock. It's funny to watch because he puts his hands on either side and tries to lift it and his arms seem like they're stretching. "It's so heavy!"

"Meteorite," I say.

He turns on the lamp next to the couch. "Metal deposits. Iron, probably."

"Yep."

He goes to lift it again, but then gives up. "This is amazing!"

"Yep," I say.

I can see him doing all kinds of math in his head.

I don't know what he's trying to figure. The weight? The value? The size of it before it hit the atmosphere? I hope we have a conversation about science and space. I hope for something that feels normal before the end of this crappy weekend.

"Is this why you said the week I left was the week we fell from space?" he asks.

I say, "The week you left we all fell from space. Now we co-own a divorce. Split four ways. You can't just pretend Jilly and I aren't in here with you. We all own it. It's ours."

"That's hard for me to agree to," he says. "You girls have nothing to do with the divorce."

"Um. We're living through it, remember?"

"True."

"And you didn't tell us about Tiffany and you never tell us how you are," I say.

"True."

"So we fell from space in January. I couldn't figure out what to do with my quarter of a divorce. I owned it but I didn't know what to do, you know? And I asked the sky what to do and the sky sent this. Like it was something we forgot. Like we fell in January, but this was our luggage. It got lost and it came in March."

Chapter 49 — Everything Is Something

Mom, Dad, Jilly, and I sit in the living room of Mom's house. This has been pre-arranged. Dad called Mom. Mom said yes. Here we are.

Jilly is feisty. She says she's fine and I think she really is. Her hamster is running around in its ball. She named it Judy.

My little meteorite is still in my pocket. I haven't named it anything.

Jilly's finished star map from January is taped to the kitchen chalkboard. She found: herself. The drawing even has pigtails like she's been wearing since summer when her hair grew out enough to make them. Mom's star map is still rolled up on the kitchen table. I guess she had a busy day.

Mom and Dad tell us about what's happening with the divorce because maybe they understand now that Jilly and I own part of it.

They tell us the paperwork should be done before the end of the year. They tell us that Dad is going to keep the every-other-weekend arrangement because it sounds like what we want. Dad says he's sorry about not telling any of us about Tiffany moving in.

Eventually, Jilly goes for her Sunday-night bath and it's just me, Mom, and Dad. They ask stuff. I try to answer.

"I'm just angry all the time," I say.

"It's okay," Dad says. "It could be a bunch of things. You've had a really hard year."

"I don't want to have to take medicine every day," I say.

"You may not have to. We have to see what the doctor says. And Jan. You'll be talking to her a lot more," Mom says.

Ugh. I feel like the world's biggest problem now.

"By the time you're in high school, you'll have a lot of coping skills. More than anyone around you. Trust me," Dad says. "Figuring this out early is so much better than figuring it out late."

"But we have to ask you a few questions just to make sure you're okay," Mom says.

I nod.

They ask me if I ever think about hurting myself. I say no. They ask me if I'm bored in school. I say no more than usual. They ask me how middle school is really going. I tell them that the vice principal said I might get to paint the science wing hallway.

"Paint it? What color?" Dad says.

I say, "Star maps, Dad. This thing happened the first week of school. I nearly got in big trouble. Long story. He likes my constellations. He was part of his astronomy club in college or something."

"That's exciting!" Mom says.

I shrug.

"You don't feel excited?" Dad asks.

I say, "There's no point in trying to get anyone to see something new in the sky. No one cares anyway."

Mom says, "What big trouble happened in school the first week? I don't remember that."

"Some girl drew a fake star map on the bathroom wall and they thought it was me." I think about how it was probably fine that she did that, considering what I did with her ring.

"You got in trouble for something you didn't do?" Dad says.

"The vice principal knew I didn't do it. The stars were all wrong."

"Can you tell me about stuff like that when it happens from now on?" Mom asks. "That way, I can help you."

We all sit there for a minute. They're looking at me and I'm looking at the rug. "Remember what you said yesterday about secrets?" I ask Mom.

She nods.

I say, "I have a secret."

Mom and Dad freeze. I can hear Jilly singing in her bath. I can hear the frogs croaking from the stream. I can hear the screech owl screeching.

"Lib?" I don't even know who says that. Mom or Dad. Maybe both of them.

"So this girl, Leah, bullied me since January. Maybe

before that. But in January—when you left," I point to Dad, "she really started saying bad stuff."

"She's the girl you called the B-word, right?" Mom says.

"Right." Dad's eyebrows go up. I guess Mom doesn't tell him everything after all. "She got everyone in sixth grade to stop talking to me." The two of them start to say things, but I ignore them. "And I really don't want to get into details but she had a diamond ring in school—it was her mom's—and I found it on the floor and I picked it up."

They look relieved already, but also concerned.

I continue. "So I couldn't give it back to her because I was scared she'd say I stole it. So I put it somewhere for safekeeping."

"Where is it now?" Mom asks.

"I gave it back to her last week."

"So you apologized?" Dad asks.

"Not quite."

They look at me. I don't know what to say.

"I got the ring back to her but she doesn't know it was me and even though she has it back, I still feel awful for not feeling guilty about it." I cry.

I know why I feel guilty. It's not for the ring. It's not even for making Jilly go get it. It's for thinking I could magically get my parents back together when really, they don't want to be together.

I can see the scene from space. I look depressed. I don't know if I really am depressed, but I know I look it.

"I can take care of the bullying thing at school. No problem," Mom says.

"I'm gonna have to tell her I had the ring," I say. "I don't want to do that right now."

"I'll be there with you. Don't worry. We'll work it out no problem," Mom says. "And next week is fine. No rush."

"What else can we do to help?" Dad asks. "We'd do anything."

I think about this.

There's nothing they can do.

They can't move time backward.

They can't be a happy family again.

They can't whisk me and Jilly off to a camping trip and pretend everything is fine.

"I have no idea," I say.

We say a few more things to each other and they hug me and tell me that they love me. This is the closest I will ever get to having what I used to have. When I think this thought, I cry so hard I can't breathe.

I feel like someone just died.

There is nothing nice about the feeling. Nothing nice about the hugs. Nothing nice about "getting my feelings out," which is what Dad whispered a second ago.

I finally figure out what to say. "Nothing will ever be good again."

They don't say anything to that. I keep crying. Dad is petting my head. Mom is rocking a little, back and forth.

I keep trying to breathe and I feel like I'm not getting enough oxygen.

Eventually, I find myself in bed. The meteorite is back in place in the corner of fluffy toys, and the house is quiet.

I whisper, "Good night, rock."

The rock doesn't answer.

A sliver of the moon is visible from my attic window.

It feels like the last time I will ever see the moon.

That's what everything feels like anymore.

Everything is something I will never see again.

Chapter 50 — Lying for Good

I'm not surprised that Mom is in the guidance office on Monday morning waiting for me. A lot happened between me leaving the house this morning and third period, which is when I was called down.

1. I tripped and fell down at the bus stop.

2. My wrist hurt so bad I had to go to the nurse.

3. I didn't want Finn Nolan to have to go through getting in trouble because he's so sad all the time, so I lied and said I tripped.

4. I don't understand #3 because he did push me and I did fall down and that's probably not a reason why I should stick up for him.

5. I have no idea why Finn pushed me. But I think I'm his toaster.

I'm lucky Mom is here because she tells the guidance

counselor that Finn and Patrick have a habit of being mean to Jilly and me.

"Did Finn say anything this morning?" Mom asks.

"No."

"Did you say anything to him?" the guidance counselor asks.

"No. I was reading a book," I say. "Crap. I think it's still at the bus stop."

"So he just pushed you? Out of the blue?" Mom asks.

"Yeah. Didn't say anything to me and I didn't say anything to him."

Something about this conversation tells me that Finn Nolan told a different story. And there is a different story. I just can't tell it.

1. Finn Nolan was already at the bus stop when I got there. I asked him how he was doing and he told me none of my business and I said that he could talk to me if he wanted to because I kinda know what he's going through and I did have my book in my hand, but I wasn't reading it, and then he pushed me and I fell.

2. My wrist hurt so bad I had to go to the nurse, but my pride hurt worse because I thought I was doing a good thing by offering Finn to be there for him when he needed it. We used to be friends.

3. I didn't tell the nurse what happened. I just started crying and the nurse asked me a bunch of questions about why I was crying and I told her that the ice wasn't helping my wrist and that it hurt so much I might die.

4. The nurse called the guidance counselor and the guidance counselor asked if I wanted to talk and I said no.

5. All the guidance counselor wanted to know was how I hurt my wrist and I finally told her that it was really Finn.

6. Mom got here and I made it sound like we didn't talk at all about anything and he just pushed me out of the blue, but he didn't. What I said really made him mad, even though I didn't say anything mean. I stuck up for Finn because he owns a quarter of a divorce just like I do and everyone pretends that because we're twelve, we can't own any part of a divorce. But we do. And I can tell he doesn't know what to do with it.

7. Mom says I need to get my wrist x-rayed. So we go to the urgent care place in town and wait.

"I don't want Finn to get in trouble," I tell Mom.
"Why not? He could have broken your wrist."

"He didn't mean to. He's just mad about stuff," I say.

"What stuff?"

"Um, you know."

"So he did talk to you?" she asks.

"He didn't say a word."

She looks at me. She has a lie detector. Some days it's faulty, and other days it's not. Today is a not-faulty day. She says, "But you said something to him, is that right?"

I hate Mom's lie detector.

I'd never thought of it the way she said it before, either. Finn may have broken my wrist. That's not good. It would get him in even more trouble. I should have just stuck with my story of tripping and falling.

"Have you connected the stars on the map I gave you yet?" I ask.

"It's a tough one," she says. "I can't find anything in there."

I start to wonder if I drew defective maps that week. I can't blame myself. It's hard drawing the stars when you're hurtling through space at hundreds of thousands of miles per hour.

Chapter 51 – What Is Finn Nolan's Toaster?

My wrist isn't broken, but it's a bad sprain. I have to wear a brace and not use it for three weeks. It's my right hand. I can't figure out how I'm supposed to live without using my right hand.

Jilly sees the brace on my wrist and the first thing she says is, "It's gonna be weird having to wipe your butt with your left hand."

When Mom tells her we're going to talk to the Nolans, she says, "Can't I stay here? Patrick is a troll."

"He won't be a troll while I'm there," Mom says.

She's wrong.

Patrick is a troll the entire time Mr. Nolan, Mom, and I talk about Finn. Finn won't come out of his room. Mr. Nolan says, "I don't know what to do with him anymore."

Mom and Mr. Nolan talk about what they can do and I go to Finn's door and knock. He says, "Go away." I knock again and say it's me. When he opens the door and sees my hand in the brace, he starts to cry into his hands.

"You don't have to hide it," I say. "I know you're sad."

"I didn't mean to push you that hard," he says. "I'm so sorry."

"I didn't want to tell anyone what happened, but the

guidance counselor hypnotized me or something," I say. "You didn't get in trouble, did you?"

"Just my dad."

"Oh," I say. This was what I wanted to save him from.

"Is it broken?"

"Just sprained," I say.

"That's good."

"Yeah."

"I can't figure out what to do to feel better," he says.

"I threw a toaster through the window."

He looks up like he doesn't believe me. "I did. Ask my mom."

"She did," Jilly says. She's standing at the doorway now.

"Stop spying," I say.

Somewhere in the house, Patrick is counting to ten. Jilly is supposed to be hiding. "Can I hide in here?" she asks.

Finn and I answer at the same time. "No!"

Jilly scampers away.

"Did you get in trouble?" Finn asks.

"A little. Not really. Everyone knew why I threw the toaster," I say. "And we didn't have to buy a new one. Robust toaster. So I had that going for me."

"Why'd you throw it?"

"I . . . I was mad," I say.

"Did it make you feel better?"

"Not really," I say. "It gets better little by little. You just have to get used to it."

"How do they expect us to get used to it?" he asks.

"I don't know. But I know it's as hard for them as it is for us."

"No. It's not. Not the same thing. Not at all." He's crying again. "Like—I get that it's hard to break up. Look at your parents. Never thought they'd break up. But then they did. It must be hard. But for us? It's like one of our parents died."

"That's the trick," I say. "They didn't die. They're both still here and we'll get to see them."

"It feels it."

"I know," I say.

"I want to run away," he says.

"Where would you go?"

"I don't know. I just want to get away from here. I hate everything."

"Me too. I hate everybody. For months. And I can't seem to tell them why," I say.

"You don't hate me," Jilly says from the doorway.

Finn and I yell back, "GO AWAY!"

Finn sits on the floor of his room, still leaking tears from his eyes. I move over and sit next to him. "Look," I say. "Maybe we can get through this together somehow. We have to go through school together anyway. We could talk or something."

"I don't want a girlfriend," Finn says.

I laugh. Can't stop myself. I just keep laughing. Finn

starts laughing too. We laugh until we're crying. Good tears. I say, "Girlfriend!" and we laugh more. As if the idea of girlfriends and boyfriends is the funniest thing in the world.

And it is.

Not just because our parents broke up. But because nobody sees how big the galaxy is when they're thinking about girlfriends and boyfriends. Earth has eight billion people on it and Leah Jones talks about how her new middle school boyfriend is her soul mate. She's in the seventh grade. I don't know why people limit themselves so much.

"Love is stupid," Finn says.

"It's probably not stupid, but I'm twelve and I don't care about it," I say.

"Is your dad different now?"

"Yeah. Pretty much," I say.

"My mom is different. She talks a lot more and she's like — a feminist or something."

"You really need to look up what that word means," I say. "It's not a bad thing."

"Let's keep talking," he says.

"Okay."

"I don't mean here. I mean at the bus stop and stuff."

"Oh good, because I can't feel my right leg and I need to get up," I say.

"I'm really sorry for that," he says, pointing to my wrist brace.

"I know."

"Sometimes I'm just so angry, it's like . . ."

"It's like a meteor hitting the atmosphere," I say.

"Something like that," he says.

"Maybe one day after school you could come over and see my meteorite," I say. "Sometimes I talk to it when I'm mad because I think it's the only thing on Earth that will understand me."

"You're weird," he says.

"Maybe you can talk to it, too."

"You don't have a meteorite," he says.

"She does!" Jilly says from the doorway. "It's big and is probably worth ten thousand dollars!"

We chase Jilly back to the kitchen where she grabs Mom and climbs onto her lap. I feel like giving Finn my pocket-meteorite but I decide I shouldn't, and it's mine.

Mr. Nolan looks nicer than he has in a long time. I don't know what Mom said to him. I say, "Finn wants to see my meteorite so tomorrow he's coming home after school with me and we can do our homework together, too."

"Sounds good," Mom says.

Mr. Nolan smirks. "You two made up quick."

"We're friends," Finn says. "Stop being weird."

Mr. Nolan stops smirking.

"I'm really sorry," Finn says again. "If you need help with anything while it heals, let me know."

Jilly looks like she's about to say something about how I have to wipe my butt with my left hand, but I shoot her a look like I'll throw a toaster at her.

....

We eat magic meatloaf for dinner.

Mom seems happier. Jilly seems fine. I feel . . . better.

When I go to bed, I ask the rock why I feel better.

"Some things take time," it says.

I think about how it takes Earth 365 days to work its way around the sun. I think about Saturn who takes 29.5 Earth *years* to make the same trip. Then Neptune: 164.9 Earth years.

I'm glad I live on Earth where things go faster.

Chapter 52 — Some Things Take Time

Jan doesn't think I have depression. Not the kind Dad has. She says we have to keep our eye on it.

"You're at the age where this shows up. Sometimes it's just ups and downs that are normal. Sometimes it's longer than that. I think you're probably depressed because you've had a sad year."

"I feel a lot better now," I say.

"What changed?"

"I was at Dad's last weekend. Then Finn sprained my wrist. This is gonna sound weird but it was like hurting my wrist helped me somehow."

"Really?"

"I could help Finn," I say. "That's what probably made me feel better."

"You can't keep focusing on other people," she says. "Plus, it's not healthy to think that helping someone who's been mean to you is a solution. Or that it's your job. That's kinda dangerous behavior, you know?"

"All boys are jerks at Finn's age."

"It's not about being a jerk. He put his hands on you. He hurt you."

"He used to be my friend. He trusted me enough to take it out on me," I say. But I hear what I said on some sort of delay and I make a face like I just ate raw clams. There is sand in my throat. "Oh my gosh. That sounded like I was defending him for hurting me."

"You *were* defending him for hurting you," Jan says.

I think about this and stare at the fluffy stuffed elephant in Jan's office. "Wow. I think I know where I learned how to do that," I say.

"I think you know, too."

"Maybe I'm more like my mom than like my dad," I say. "Maybe I'm making excuses for people who aren't nice because it's a way to keep the peace or something."

"It's a hard habit to break, but we'll break it together," Jan says.

"I'm still so sad, though."

"That's normal. You found out a lot of new stuff this weekend. That kind of information takes time to process," she says.

Jan tells me that divorce causes similar emotional reactions as death. It's mourning. There are stages. She says there are a ton of different types of depression, too. There's sadness about a situation, there's "feeling depressed," which can last longer, and then there's the disease of depression, which can be all kinds of different things.

I'm scared of getting what Dad has, but I also know that he can be happy, too. Depression can do a lot of awful

255

things, but Jan says it can also help me be very aware of how I'm feeling and that's super important.

"A lot of people don't know how they're feeling," I say.

"That's true."

"My feelings showed up in my star maps, mostly."

"Then keep drawing them," she says.

I decide that tonight would be a good night to go up to the hill.

....

When we get home, Mom shows me her finished star map from January. She's connected the dots into camping tools. A hatchet, a bowie knife, a tent, a campfire, and something that looks like a marshmallow. I guess the stars show you what's on your mind, just like I always thought. And it's October, Mom's favorite camping season.

I call Dad when I get home but his number goes to his voicemail, so I leave a message. "Hi, Dad. I read your letter again today. I want you to know you're a great dad. That's all. And tonight I'm going up to the hill to make a new map. Figured you'd want to know that. I love you."

....

I take my wrist brace off so I can hold my pencil. Mom says it's okay to take it off sometimes. It gets stiff if I don't.

Up here on the hill, there's a breeze, while the rest of Lou's woods feel like they moved to Florida. It's October. It shouldn't be this warm.

I lay my blanket out and wait for the show. It's dusk now and the sky is turning dark purple.

I put my headlamp on my head and test to see if the batteries are still good. They are. For a minute, I feel like nothing has changed. But of course, everything has changed.

My parents are planets who are no longer aligned.

Dad lives with Tiffany now—a new planet we never knew about before. It's exciting if you look at it that way.

Jilly is still Venus and I'm still Mars except I'm not glowing a faint red anymore because I threw a toaster out a window. Or because of something. I'm not sure why. Some things take time.

But the batteries in my headlamp didn't know any of this was going on and they still work just fine. Same as billions of other people who didn't fall from space this year. They work just fine.

....

Jupiter is the first thing I see. I smile. It's following the moon in the southern sky.

Sometimes I can't believe I can look up at the sky and see these things. Planets. Meteors. Stars. It's all magic, really.

More stars appear as the sky gets darker.

I wish on the first one.

Vega.

There's something special about Vega but I don't know what. If a star can be friendly to a human, then Vega feels friendly toward me. If a star can suddenly become my best friend, then Vega has just become my best friend. I know that makes me sound weird, but I'm weird, so I don't mind.

Even if you call me weird to my face, I can still show you which way is north.

If you want, we can hang out with my meteorite.

If you think you've fallen from space, then you will feel at home with us.

....

I draw my star map—the first real one since I threw the toaster—and I don't stop. I just keep drawing star after star. No shapes yet, but they'll come.

When I draw, I don't think of the stars like a map of our town anymore. I gave up on being Polaris because it's too much work pointing strangers in the right direction. I have to find the right direction myself.

I don't know what time it is and Mom hasn't called me in yet, so I don't care what time it is. The stars are everywhere. The sky is packed with them. It feels like there are more than I've ever seen.

I stop drawing and lie back and marvel at it all.

The screech owl screeches. The frogs are still going because it's warm out here, October or not. The sky is peaceful. I feel peaceful, too, somehow. I'm still scared and pretty sad, but something about today made me feel like I'm really on Earth again and not falling through space.

Since I threw the toaster, the stars didn't feel as dependable as they used to, but tonight, they feel the way they did when I was little and Dad explained, "The sky goes around and around Polaris, like a top that spins forever."

That's the thing about the stars.

They're always here. They're the most trustworthy friends. They will always be exactly where they're supposed to be at the time they're supposed to be there. They can lead you home. They just keep going around and around.

There are 108 days until the anniversary of Dad moving out.

The stars will be in the exact same place as they were last year, but the planets will have moved. Just like Dad did. Just like I did. Just like Jilly did. Just like Mom did.

Planets have their own course.

But no matter what happens, the world keeps turning and the stars will be there in the same place you left them only a year ago.

Nothing else on Earth is like this.

Nothing else is as trustworthy.

Nothing else can make you as small as the stars. As big as the stars.

Jan told me today that I didn't have to talk with Leah Jones yet. She said I could wait a week or two. She said she wanted to talk to me about it more before then. I'll tell her that I didn't feel bad for hiding Leah's ring and how that scared me. I'll tell her about how I wasn't ever fine when I said I was fine. I'll tell her how I became a meteor. How I made a deal with the stars. How the stars didn't keep their promise and how I knew that they were never going to. I'll tell her that I am learning how to forgive Dad for his mistakes. I'll tell her that I am learning to forgive myself, too. I'll tell her how the sky puts everything in perspective.

How it makes me happy.

How I'm an exciting exception.

I'm Liberty Johansen—the girl who will change the way human beings look at the night sky. They will see their lives drawn out above them every night if they want.

The sky is free. That's what I'll tell them.

The pictures in it are your own. That's what they'll discover if they look up long enough.

Draw often. You don't get good at anything by only doing it once or twice, I'll say.

Some things take time.

Author's Note

It takes a whole lot of people to make a book. Did you know that? Sure, I write the thing, but when I send it to my publisher, it's like I'm part of the best kickball team ever. To the entire squad at Arthur A. Levine Books: thank you. Galaxy-sized shout-out to my editor, Nick Thomas, who is incurably rad.

Still trending: Michael Bourret is the best agent ever. (Thank you, Michael.)

Readers—be you students or teachers or anything in between—thank you for reading, for writing to me, and for being so honest in our conversations.

Thank you to Livy and Topher King, who support me every day, and to Gracie, who was this book's first reader and who has been and forever will be the fuel behind my fiery advocacy for early and comprehensive mental and emotional health discussion and education.

You must understand, reader—you matter. And how you feel matters. And talking is actually your star map. It's how you find your way.

Finally, if you like stars and constellations and haven't downloaded Stellarium yet, do it! It's free and it's so amazing to see the stars and planets and all the other great things in the sky in real time.

https://stellarium.org/

AMY SARIG KING is the author of *Me and Marvin Gardens*, a *Washington Post* Best Book of the Year and Texas Bluebonnet Master List selection. She has also published many critically acclaimed young adult novels under the name A.S. King, including *Please Ignore Vera Dietz*, which was named a Michael L. Printz Honor Book, *Ask the Passengers*, which won the *Los Angeles Times* Book Prize, and, most recently, *Dig*. She lives in southeastern Pennsylvania, with her family.

Visit her website at as-king.com and follow her on Twitter at @AS_King.